Once Upon a Fairytale

Whisked away into a world of fantasy and romance...

In these contemporary love stories inspired by enchanting classic fairytales, a happily-ever-after ending is in store for two gorgeous couples!

Discover Gabrielle and Deacon's story in

Beauty and Her Boss

Could Gabrielle be the one to bring light into Deacon's locked-away heart?

Available now!

And read Sage and Quinton's story, the next book in the duet, coming soon!

Dear Reader,

Welcome to the first book in the Once Upon a Fairytale duet. Deacon and Gabrielle's story is loosely based on one of my favorite stories, *Beauty and the Beast*.

Gabrielle Dupré would do anything for her father—even if it means sacrificing her happiness to protect him from his own foolishness. She's a hard worker, trying to keep their heads above financial waters, but it isn't easy. And when the death of a family member sends her father into a tailspin, it's up to Gabrielle to fix things...if only she can reason with the beast.

Not so long ago, Deacon Santoro was Hollywood's sexiest actor. And then one night, a horrific car accident changed everything. Since then he has secluded himself in his Malibu mansion. The accident has left him with blanks in his memory, leaving him to guess at what happened that fateful night. However, the paparazzi and a multitude of people have prematurely convicted him.

When a demonstration outside his mansion leads him to deal with Gabrielle, he's not in the mood to negotiate—until he learns she's the niece of the woman who died in the accident. That changes absolutely everything. The woman's final wish was for him to care for Gabrielle. Now he must honor that request. But will the price be too high? Or will this beauty find a way to tame the beast?

Happy reading,

Jennifer Faye

Beauty and Her Boss

Jennifer Faye

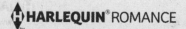

Recycling programs
for this product may
not exist in your area.

ISBN-13: 978-1-335-13504-9

Beauty and Her Boss

First North American publication 2018

Copyright © 2018 by Jennifer F. Stroka

Printed in U.S.A.

Award-winning author **Jennifer Faye** pens fun, heartwarming contemporary romances with rugged cowboys, sexy billionaires and enchanting royalty. Internationally published, with books translated into nine languages, she is a two-time winner of the *RT Book Reviews* Reviewers' Choice Award. She has also won the CataRomance Reviewers' Choice Award, been named a Top Pick! author and been nominated for numerous other awards.

Books by Jennifer Faye

Harlequin Romance

Mirraccino Marriages

The Millionaire's Royal Rescue
Married for His Secret Heir

Brides for the Greek Tycoons

The Greek's Ready-Made Wife
The Greek's Nine-Month Surprise

The Vineyards of Calanetti

Return of the Italian Tycoon

The Prince's Christmas Vow
Her Festive Baby Bombshell
Snowbound with an Heiress

Visit the Author Profile page
at Harlequin.com for more titles.

PROLOGUE

"THIS CAN'T BE HAPPENING."

Gabrielle Dupré frowned as she perched on the edge of a hard, black plastic chair. The room was small with gray walls. Outside the little room, there was the buzz of voices and phones ringing. But inside the room, a tense silence hung in the air like a dense fog. This was a place she'd never been in her life—a police station. How had things spiraled so far out of control? Her head pounded and her stomach churned.

After being here for more than two hours, the situation wasn't looking good. Not good at all. She'd just played her final card and she'd been praying ever since that it would pay off.

"Don't worry, daughter." Her father stared at her from across a black nondescript table. "Everything will be all right."

"All right?" She struggled not to shout in frustration. "Things are so far from all right."

With each word, her voice crept up in volume. Realizing that losing her cool right now would not help their cause, she paused and swallowed hard. "Father, do you know how much trouble you're in?"

"Gaby, don't you understand? If I got word out about that monster, then it was worth it." His voice was filled with conviction. "Sometimes a man has to do what he has to do."

"And sometimes he needs to think before he acts," she said in a heated whisper. Anger pulsed through her veins, but it wasn't her father that she was upset with—it was herself.

Her father reached out and patted her hand. "You'll see. This will all work out."

She blamed herself for not being there to reason with her father. And to stop him from acting rashly. For the past six months, she'd been working two jobs to pay their outstanding bills but she was still losing financial ground. Things were so bad she was considering taking on a third job. With her father's health declining and him now in a wheelchair, it was up to her to make ends meet.

And through it all, she'd made sure to be there for her father every single day. He had been grieving ever since her aunt's deadly car accident almost four months ago. And it didn't help that the police had failed to release the truth about the accident. Although, that didn't stop the gossip sites from pointing fingers, including the magazine she'd recently started doing an admin job for, *QTR*. By way of some unnamed source, they were accusing an award-winning movie star, Deacon Santoro, of being at fault.

Gaby was still trying to figure out the how and why of her father's actions. "So you've been sneaking off to Deacon Santoro's estate all week?"

His gaze narrowed. "I wasn't sneaking. I didn't want to bother you so I took the bus."

She shook her head in disbelief. "I thought you had a girlfriend that you weren't ready to tell me about. If I'd have known what you were up to, I would have stopped you."

With her father's elbows resting on the table, he leaned toward her. His bloodshot eyes pleaded with her. "Don't you want the truth?"

"Of course I do. How could you question that? I loved her, too. She was like a second mother to me. But there are better ways to get to the truth. You shouldn't have staged a loud, disruptive protest in front of the man's house and accosted his staff."

Her father expelled a heavy sigh as he leaned back in his wheelchair. "Nothing else has worked. I've made phone call after phone call to the authorities. All I get is the runaround. They keep saying the accident report will be released as soon as the investigation has been completed."

Gaby couldn't believe what she was about to say, but someone had to reason with her father. With her mother and now her aunt gone, the responsibility landed squarely on Gabrielle's straining shoulders.

"Do you even realize how much power Mr. Santoro wields?"

Her father's bushy, gray eyebrows drew together. "Why do you think I went there? The police aren't helping us get the truth because he bought them off."

Gaby shushed her father. "Don't say those things."

"So I thought the media might help. After all, they'd do anything for a big headline."

"You certainly got their attention." Sadly, she didn't think this tactic was going to work, but she sure hoped she was wrong because the not knowing was eating at her, too. "There were so many reporters standing outside the police station that I had to be escorted through the back entrance."

Her father's tired face, with its two days' worth of stubble, lifted into a satisfied smile. "It's working. You'll see."

Her father had a bad habit of acting first and thinking later. And she was left with the task of cleaning up his messes. But this was his first and, if she had any say in it, his last arrest. "And is it worth you going to jail or paying a stiff fine that will financially wipe us out?"

Before her father could answer, the door swung open. A tall police officer with salt-and-pepper hair stepped just inside the room. "We've contacted the complainant."

"And…" Gaby knew this was the time for restraint but there was so much on the line.

The officer shook his head. "He refused to meet with you."

That was not what she'd wanted to hear. She was hoping to plead with the man and hopefully get him to drop the charges. Her father was not physically well and punishing him would not help anyone, least of all Deacon Santoro. "Surely there has to be some way I can speak with him."

The officer cleared his throat. "I was about to tell you that he's on the phone. You may speak with him at my desk."

That was all the invitation she needed. In a heartbeat, she was on her feet and rushing out the door. She didn't so much as pause to assure her father that she'd straighten out this mess—because in all honesty, she wasn't sure she could fix things this time. But she was willing to do anything to protect her father—even from his own misguided sense of justice.

The police officer led her to his desk, where he handed over the receiver. Before she got a word out, the officer was called away to help with an unruly arrestee, who appeared intoxicated and quite belligerent.

Turning her back to the scene, Gaby said, "Hello."

"I am not dropping the charges." Deacon Santoro didn't even so much as utter a greeting, friendly or otherwise.

And yet his voice caught her attention. It was deep and rich, like a fine bourbon. She didn't need to verify who she was speaking to. After watching each and every one of his movies countless times, she would recognize Deacon's voice anywhere.

"I would really appreciate if we could talk this out."

"I've done all of the talking that I intend to do." His sexy voice was short and clipped. "Now, I've spoken to you. That is all I agreed to. I must go—"

"Wait!"

"This is a waste of time. Your father is guilty. He will have to take it up with the judge."

With each syllable the man spoke, her body betrayed her by being drawn in by the deep timbre of his voice. Logic dictated that he was the absolute last person she should be fantasizing about, but there was another more primal part of her that wanted to hear his voice again.

Gaby gave herself a swift mental jerk. She had to stay on point. Her father's future was depending on her getting this right.

"But he didn't do anything serious—"

"I'd call stalking a serious charge."

"Stalking?" This was the first she'd heard of this allegation. She couldn't help but wonder what else her father had failed to tell her.

"Yes. He's been making harassing phone calls, skulking outside my residence with binoculars and hounding my entire staff."

"I'm sorry. He hasn't been himself lately. He wouldn't hurt a soul. If you knew him—"

"I don't. And I don't plan to. None of this is my problem."

Mr. Santoro was right on that point, but would it hurt him to be a little generous? Perhaps she needed to explain the situation better. "My father, he isn't young. And his health is failing."

"Again, not my problem."

This man wasn't going to give an inch. His stirring voice ceased to affect her as she went into protective mode. "Listen, Mr. Santoro, I am sorry for the trouble my father has caused you, but pressing charges against him won't fix anything. Surely there has to be another way to work this out."

"Your father should have thought of all of this before he decided to cause trouble for me."

Why did this man have to act as though he was the innocent party here? If it weren't for his actions on that fateful night, her father wouldn't have bothered him. Angry accusations bubbled up within her and hovered at the back of her throat. It would be so easy to lose her cool—to tell this man exactly what she thought of him, which wasn't much.

What good would that do her? Yes, it'd temporarily make her feel better.

But in the long term, would it do anything to help her father? Definitely not.

Gaby's jaw muscles clenched. Her back teeth ground together.

"If that's all, I must go."

"It's not all." He wasn't getting off that easy. "My father was doing what he thought was best for my aunt."

"What does your aunt have to do with this? Or was she one of those misguided people that he coerced into shouting lies and throwing garbage onto my property?"

Gaby wasn't going to let this man go on about her father and aunt. Did he really not know who her father was? "My aunt wasn't outside your house. She—she died in the car accident."

There was a swift intake of breath as though at last he understood the gravity of the situation. A long silence ensued. Was it possible she'd finally gotten through to him?

Still, she didn't breathe easy—not yet. In just the short period of time that she'd spoken with this man, she'd learned that he didn't change his mind easily. And yet, she couldn't give up.

Every muscle in his body tensed.

Deacon Santoro didn't utter a word as he processed this new piece of information. How was this the first he'd heard of the woman in the accident having a family?

He searched his impaired memory for an answer. And then he latched on to the vital information. The police had said the woman had no family—no living parents, no ex-spouses and no children. Just a surviving brother. Deacon had never thought to ask about nieces and nephews.

Deacon swallowed hard. "You're her niece?"

"Yes. My name's Gaby."

"As in Gabrielle?"

"Yes. My aunt was the only one who called me Gabrielle."

Take care of Gabrielle.

Those words haunted him each night in his short and troubled sleep. Until now, he'd never understood what they meant. He didn't know anyone named Gabrielle. But suddenly a jagged piece of a memory from the accident came back to him. It wasn't an image but rather a voice. The woman from the accident had told him to take care of her niece.

And it was his chance to make sure the woman's final words were fulfilled. The need to help Gabrielle was overwhelming. But how? He needed time to absorb this revelation—to form a viable plan.

Deacon cleared his throat. "I didn't know she was your aunt. No one told me."

"Now you can understand my father's actions. He's grieving for his younger sister. He isn't thinking clearly."

"But that still doesn't make up for what he's cost me." Thanks to her father, another in a string of employees had quit. And thanks to the negative publicity, associates were shying away from doing business with him.

"I will do whatever I can to make this right."

He applauded her for trying to clean up a

mess that wasn't hers. "How much are you talking about?"

"You want money?" Her voice took on a note of distress.

No. He had enough of his own, but he didn't want this conversation to end—not until he knew a bit more about this woman. "You did offer to make things right and I lost a lot of money when two promising business ventures fell through thanks to your father's actions."

"I—I don't have any money. Please believe me. I work two jobs to keep us afloat."

"Us?" The word rolled off his tongue before he could stop it. Suddenly he pictured this woman with a husband and children—her own support system.

"Yes. Me and my father."

At this point, Deacon should just hang up, but he couldn't do it. The father may have stepped over the line, but the daughter hadn't. And those words kept haunting him—*take care of Gabrielle.*

"What do you have in mind?" he asked.

"I could go outside and talk to the media. I could explain my father's actions—"

"Don't. The less said the better." All the while, he was considering how best to help this woman, who obviously had too much on her plate.

"So if my father and I agree not to say another word, you will see that the charges are dropped?"

"No. Not only has my name been slandered in the news, but my assistant was coming back from lunch when your father's protest was at its height. She was verbally assaulted and had things thrown at her. She has quit. And the temp agency doesn't want to send anyone else."

"Oh." Gabrielle paused. "I don't know what you want me to do to make this right."

"You don't need to do anything. You did not cause this mess." Something told him this wasn't Gabrielle's first time cleaning up after her father. Perhaps taking care of Gabrielle meant freeing her from being constantly at her father's beck and call. "Your father must face up to what he's done."

"But he's in no physical condition to go through the legal process—"

"This isn't your first time fixing things for your father, is it?"

"No." She quickly added, "But he needs me."

"Your father, can he cook for himself?"

"Yes, but—"

"Do his own laundry and shopping?"

"Yes, but—"

"You do most everything for him, don't you?"

"Of course I do. I'm his daughter. Now tell me what I can do to remedy things."

In that moment, Deacon knew what needed to be done. Without giving himself a chance to back out, he said, "There is one thing and it's nonnegotiable."

"Name it."

"Come work for me."

CHAPTER ONE

Two days later...

WHAT EXACTLY HAD she agreed to?

Gabrielle Dupré's heart beat faster as she turned into the gated drive of the Santoro estate. Her gaze shifted to the clock on the dash. The drive from Bakersfield had taken more than four hours. She definitely wouldn't want to deal with that long commute each day. Thankfully Newton, an old friend from the neighborhood, had recently moved back to town and was renting a room from her father and had agreed to keep an eye on him while she worked here at the estate. Newton had changed since she'd last seen him, but he was happy to be there for her father, and they seemed to get on.

Deacon had offered her more money to work here than both of her jobs combined. It also included free room and board. Under different circumstances, she'd be excited about the opportunity. But with her father convinced that Mr. Santoro was the reason her aunt had died, being here felt uncomfortable to say the least.

She swallowed hard and reached out the driver's side window, pressing a finger to a button on the intercom. She waited for someone to speak to her. However, without a word the gate swept open. She had to admit she was curious to see what awaited her on the other side of the wall. She'd done an internet search, but it hadn't turned up any pictures of the estate.

Gabrielle eased her father's vintage red convertible onto the overgrown grounds. It certainly wasn't the grand estate that she'd been anticipating. Perhaps at one time this place might have been beautiful, but now it was woefully neglected. The grass appeared not to have been cut in ages. The bushes were overgrown and gangly. The flower gardens were overrun with weeds that were strangling out the few remaining flowers.

The internet sites said that Deacon Santoro had become a recluse since he'd been involved in the deadly accident. Apparently for once, the paparazzi hadn't been totally wrong. There was definitely something amiss on this estate.

The Malibu beach house was a stunning piece of midcentury architecture. Gabrielle slowed the car to a stop to have a better look around. Feeling as though someone was staring at her, she glanced up at the massive white mansion. There was no one standing in any of the windows. But there was a window on the top floor where the sheers moved. Cold fingertips inched down her spine.

Stop it. You're just being melodramatic. It's not like this is a haunted mansion.

No matter what she told herself, she couldn't shake her uneasiness. If it wasn't for her father, she'd turn around and leave. But a deal was a deal.

When she'd handed in her immediate resignation at the library, they'd refused to accept it. The staff was small and they were all close, like a family. So, she was on sabbatical leave until her deal with Deacon was concluded. She was so grateful to have a job to return to. It was one less thing she had to worry about.

However, when she'd resigned at the tabloid, she'd made the mistake of letting Deacon Santoro's name cross her lips. That spiked everyone's interest. She'd been passed up the chain of management until she'd been sitting across from the managing editor. And when the whole sordid truth came tumbling out, the editor had assured her that she didn't need to quit. In fact, they'd increased her pay.

The editor was putting Gaby on an assignment. The money was most welcome as her father's mounting medical expense were beyond her means. She had been shocked until it became clear that they wanted her to feed them every bit of dirt she could dig up on Deacon Santoro. She'd initially refused. Finding out the truth about her aunt's death was one thing. Digging up information about his private life just for sensational headlines was something else.

In the end, they'd all agreed that she would remain on the payroll and submit a daily report with information regarding the deadly accident. After all, if the legal system wouldn't do anything about it, someone had to seek justice in whatever way possible. And so Gaby had come here not only to protect her father, but also to uncover the truth about the accident and to expose Deacon's actions to the world.

At the time, the plan had seemed so easy. She'd play along as his assistant and befriend the man, which from the looks of the desolate place wouldn't be hard. Then she'd get him to open up about the accident. She would prove that he was responsible for her aunt's death. At last the world would know the truth, just like her father had wanted for so long. And then she could return to her life—a life that was temporarily on pause.

Gabrielle wheeled the car into a parking spot next to a late model gray sedan. She'd arrived early this morning as she'd wanted to make a good impression on Mr. Santoro. She didn't want to give him any reason to go back on his agreement to drop the charges against her father, and that included keeping her connection with *QTR* magazine hush-hush.

She climbed out of the car and lifted her head to the blue sky. There was a gusty breeze. The forecasters said there was a storm brewing over the Pacific, although it hadn't reached them yet. But there was an ominous tension in the air.

She turned to head inside, but she wasn't sure where to go. There was yet another fence surrounding the building. There were numerous gates but no signs indicating where each led.

A movement in the corner of her eye caught her attention. Her gaze strayed across the outline of a figure in the distance.

"Excuse me," Gabrielle called out as she rushed forward.

The man's back was to her.

She called out again.

The man straightened from where he was

bent over a rosebush. He was wearing jeans, a black long-sleeved shirt and a ball cap. He didn't turn around. Did he hear her?

"Hey, could you tell me where to go?" Not about to continue screaming across the grounds, she started down to a set of stained concrete steps leading to the garden.

By the time she reached the bottom step, the man was gone. Perhaps he hadn't heard her. He could still be around here somewhere. She started walking around in hopes of spotting him again. However, he was nowhere to be found. How was that possible? He was just here a second ago. She turned around in a circle. Where had he gone so quickly?

She sighed and was about to walk away when she paused to take in her surroundings. She stood on the edge of an expansive rose garden with a winding footpath. Unlike the rest of the overgrown yard, this section was neat and tidy. She found this shocking. What made this garden so special? It was just one more question that she had for Mr. Santoro.

Gaby headed back up the steps to the parking area. If worse came to worse, she would try all the gates and open all of the doors she encountered until she found where she belonged. You really would think Mr. Santoro would greet her or at the very least call her.

Time was getting away from her. If she didn't hurry, she was going to start off this arrangement by being late. Talk about making a bad situation worse. She picked up her pace.

At the top of the steps, she glanced around. On both sides of the parking area were doors. There was the large main house and there were six garage doors with what appeared to be a guesthouse atop them. Would he have put the office in the guesthouse?

Her gaze moved back and forth between the two structures as she tried to make up her mind. Just as she decided to try the main house, a gate swung open. At last, Mr. Santoro had come to greet her.

She rushed toward the door, but she came to a halt when an older woman with white hair and a round, rosy face came hurrying out. The woman was muttering something under her breath and shaking her head, but Gaby wasn't able to make out what she was saying.

When the woman's gaze met hers, a smile softened the woman's face. She had kind eyes and a warm smile. "Ah…hello, dearie. You must be Mr. Santoro's new assistant."

Gaby smiled back at the woman. "I am. My name's Gaby Dupré."

"Welcome Ms. Dupré. And you can call me Mrs. Kupps. Mr. Santoro, he likes formality."

"I'm pleased to meet you, Mrs. Kupps." Gaby held out her hand to the woman. "But please feel free to call me Gaby."

The woman giggled and placed her hand in Gaby's for a brief shake. "I'm pleased to meet you, too," she whispered, "Gaby."

"Will you be showing me what I need to do?"

The woman shook her head. "Not me, dearie. I wouldn't have a clue. I'm the housekeeper and cook."

Gaby was disappointed. Working with Mrs. Kupps would have certainly made her workday interesting. "Do you know who will be showing me what I need to do?"

"I assume that would be Mr. Santoro."

"Oh, will he be out soon?"

The woman clucked her tongue. "Mr. Santoro does not get out much these days."

"Not even on his own estate?"

The woman shook her head as a serious look came over her face. "He prefers to stay in his suite of rooms."

This arrangement was getting stranger by the minute.

"But how will I be able to work with him?"

"He will phone you."

And then Mrs. Kupps pointed out the way to the office. Gaby made it there with ease. Once inside, she glanced around the office, taking in the white walls and two desks that faced each other from across the room. They were both sparsely set up, but the one to her left looked a bit haphazard, as though the person had been in a rush to get out the door.

The room was adorned with beach decorations and a couple of prints of the ocean. It was pretty, but there was nothing of the man that owned this spacious estate. There were no movie posters, no snapshots of Mr. Santoro with costars and no awards. It was though he'd purposely removed himself from the room. But why?

Gaby moved to one of the desks and placed her purse as well as her pink-and-white tote on the desk chair. Her gaze scanned the desk as she searched for any instructions of what was expected of her or a number that she was supposed to call upon arrival.

Then the phone rang.

He should have never agreed to bring Gabrielle here.

The decision had been made in haste.

And it was a mistake.

Deacon paced back and forth in his private study. This woman with the honeyed voice was dangerous, as she was poised to be a distraction from the stark reality of his situation. She would make him think about all of the damage that had been done. If only he could remember the accident—remember if he was at fault.

He would need to be on constant guard around her. With her being the niece of the woman who had died in his arms, she would be out to finish what her father started—destroying him.

And then he'd almost been caught by Gabrielle while he was in the rose garden.

It was his oasis. His chance to feel like a normal person, not a man hunted and hounded for the truth—something he didn't possess. How exactly had she missed the sign that explicitly said Do Not Enter?

Luckily he'd had enough time to make a clean escape. But as her sweet voice called out to him, he'd hesitated. An overwhelming urge came over him to capture a glimpse of the face that went with such a melodious voice.

In the shadows, he paused and turned back. He'd been awestruck. He didn't know how long he'd stood there in the shadows watching her move about the garden searching for him. Her long hair had bounced around her slim shoulders. Her face—it was captivating. It wasn't the type of beauty that was created with powder and makeup. No. Hers was a natural, undeniable beauty.

Her creamy complexion was flawless. He was too far away to catch the color of her eyes. He imagined they would be blue. His gaze strayed down past her pert nose and paused on her lush, rosy lips. Oh, she was definitely going to be a big distraction.

He jerked his meandering thoughts to an immediate halt. What was done, was done, as his mother would say. Now he had to deal with the consequences.

Deacon Santoro gripped the phone in his good hand and pressed the number for the office. He lifted the receiver to his ear. Two rings later, Gabrielle answered. The tone of her voice was a sweet blend of vanilla and caramel with a touch of honey.

He did not have time to get caught up in such nonsense.

Focus.

Deacon resumed pacing. "I see you decided to abide by our agreement."

"I don't see how I had any choice?"

"Everybody has choices—"

"Not in this case."

"And you were able to find someone to check in on your father?" He didn't know why he'd asked except that when he'd first made this proposal, Gabrielle had been quite hesitant to leave her father.

"I have a friend staying with him. Newton just moved back to the area and my father had a spare room. It seemed like a good idea at the time."

"I take it you've since changed your mind about this Newton."

Gabrielle hesitated. "Let's just say I've gotten to know him better and he's not the same as I remembered."

"I see." Deacon's curiosity spiked, but he forced himself to drop the Newton subject. "At least you won't have to worry about your father."

Deacon was impressed by her allegiance to her father, but that wouldn't be enough to sway him to concede. Her father had cost him more than just bad press, a mess in his yard and upset employees—her father had stirred up the paparazzi. Once again, there were news reports on television and the internet. His phone—with its private number—was now receiving calls from journalists wanting "the truth."

The little sleep he did get was once again riddled with nightmares—fiery, jagged dreams. But when he woke up, the images blurred and the memories receded to the back of his mind. With each dream, he hoped he'd be able to latch on to the elusive truth of what happened on that deadly night. But try as he might, his memory had holes the size of craters and images blurred as if in a dense fog.

The doctors had warned him that the memories might never come back to him. That was not the answer he'd wanted to hear. He needed the truth—even if it meant he was responsible for taking another person's life. Trying to live with the unknown was a torture that had him knotted up inside.

"If you would just tell me where to meet you, we can sit down and go over what is expected of me." Gabrielle's voice cut through his thoughts.

"That won't be necessary."

"Of course it is."

He could hear the confusion in her voice. She wasn't the first assistant that had been uncomfortable with his distant style of management, but it was the way it had to be. He didn't need anyone eyeing him with pity. He didn't deserve anyone feeling sorry for him. It was best for him to keep to the shadows. The accident had left permanent scars on him both inside and out. His career as an actor was over. And he was now struggling to find a new position for himself in the background of Hollywood.

He cleared his throat. "All of your instructions are on your computer. The password is capital B-e-a-c-h."

"Will you be stopping by the office later?"

"No."

"I don't understand—"

"We will conduct our business via the phone or preferably by email."

"But what if I have papers for you to sign? Or mail. I'm assuming that I'll be receiving your business correspondence."

"You will. And if you check next to the interior door, there is a mail slot. Drop whatever correspondence needs my attention in there and I'll get to it."

"But that doesn't seem very efficient. I don't mind bringing it to you—"

"No!" His voice vibrated with emotion. He clenched his jaw and swallowed hard. He didn't want to have to explain himself. After all, he was the boss. In a calmer voice, he said, "This is the arrangement. If you don't like it, you are free to leave. Our deal will be null and void."

"And my father?"

"He will face the judge and pay for the trouble he caused."

"No. I can do this." Her words were right, but her voice lacked conviction.

In all honesty, if she quit, he didn't know

what he'd do for help. The temp agencies
had blacklisted him after he'd gone through
a dozen temps in the past couple of months.
But he'd make do, one way or the other. He always had in the past. "You're sure?"

"I am."

"Then I will let you review the document
that I've emailed you. It should explain everything including the fact that I work late into
the night, but I don't expect you to. However,
I will have work waiting for you each morning." When sleep evaded him, he found it best
to keep his mind busy. It kept the frustration
and worries of the unknown at bay.

"Does anyone else work in the office?" she
asked.

"No."

She didn't immediately respond.

He hadn't considered that she wouldn't like
working alone. It had been one of his require-
ments through the temp agencies, but Gabrielle hadn't given him time to get in to specifics
when they'd spoken on the phone. Maybe this
was his way out—even if the voice inside his
head kept saying that he needed to watch out
for her.

He cleared his throat. "If working alone is
going to be a problem, we could end this now."

The silence on her end continued. He really wished he could look into her eyes. For the first time, he found communicating via the phone frustrating.

"No. It won't be a problem." Her voice sounded confident. "But I have a stipulation of my own."

"And that would be?"

"I need to speak with my father at least once a day—"

"That's fine."

"Would you reconsider letting me visit him? He will miss me."

This separation was to punish her father— not her. He'd cost Deacon and now the man had to pay a price—even if it wasn't dictated by a judge. Her father would learn not to take Gabrielle for granted.

"He should have thought of that before he allowed you to pay the price for his actions. Our arrangement will hold. You will stay here and work for three months."

Deacon knew what it was like to be alone. Both of his parents had passed on and he had no siblings. Other than Mrs. Kupps, the house-keeper, he was alone in this big rambling estate—except now Gabrielle was here. And somehow her mere presence seemed to make this place a little more appealing and less like a prison.

"My father didn't make me do anything. I volunteered." Her indignation came through loud and clear.

"Now that everything is settled, I'll let you get to work." Deacon disconnected the call.

Something told him this was going to be a very, very long three months. But it definitely wouldn't be boring.

CHAPTER TWO

THIS DEFINITELY WASN'T her best first day on the job.

In fact, it ranked right up there as one of the worst.

And the day wasn't over yet.

A loud crack of thunder shook the windows at the same time as lightning lit up the sky around the guesthouse. Gabrielle rushed to close the French doors. Somehow the weather seemed rather fitting.

She had one more piece of business before she curled up with a book and escaped from reality. She had to file her first report with *QTR*.

Gaby sat down at the granite kitchen bar and opened her laptop. She stared at a blank screen with the cursor blinking at her...mocking her. What would she say? She didn't even know what format to use. Did they expect her to tell a story or stick to bullet points?

Sure, she'd earned a bachelor's degree in

journalism, but with a downturn in the economy, she hadn't been able to land a position in publishing, so she'd returned to school. She'd gone on to get a second degree in library science. Books had always been her first love.

And as much as she loved words, right now they wouldn't come to her. She typed a couple of words, but they didn't sound right. She deleted them.

This is ridiculous. It's not an article for the public to read. It doesn't have to be perfect. It just needs to be the facts. So start writing.

The man has closed himself completely off from others. Is it the result of guilt? Or something else?

As she pressed Enter to begin the next point, the landline rang. That was odd. She hadn't given anyone that phone number. Her father had her cell phone number.

She picked up the phone. "Hello."

"Did you find everything you need?" Not a greeting. Just straight to the point.

"Yes, I did."

"I wasn't sure what you like to eat, so I had Mrs. Kupps prepare you a plate of pasta, a tossed salad and some fresh baked bread. You will find it in your kitchen."

Outside the storm raged on with thunder and howling wind. Gaby did her best to ignore it. "Thank you." Had he called purely out of courtesy? Or was this his way of checking up on her? Perhaps this was her opportunity to flush him out of the shadows. "Will you be joining me?"

"No." His voice was firm and without hesitation. He was certainly a stubborn man. "In the future, you can let Mrs. Kupps know what you eat and don't eat, so that she can plan the menu appropriately."

"I—I can do that." She hesitated. "The guesthouse is nice." There was some sort of grunt on his end of the phone. She wasn't sure what it was supposed to mean, so she ignored it. "What time would you like to get started in the morning?"

"I start before the sun is up. You can start by eight. Will that be a problem?"

"No. Not at all." She was used to opening the library at eight each morning. "I have a few things that I'd like to go over with you. Shall we meet in my office?"

"I thought you understood that this arrangement is to be by phone or email. I don't do one-on-one meetings—"

"But—"

"There are no exceptions. Good night."

And with that terse conclusion, he'd hung up on her. She stared at the phone. She could not believe that this man was so stubborn. Working for him was going to be difficult, but trying to get information about the accident from him was going to be downright impossible—unless she could get past this wall between them. And she hadn't come this far to give up.

Gaby hung up the phone and turned her attention back to the report for *QTR*. She'd lost her concentration after speaking with Deacon. She was back to staring at the blinking cursor and wondering what she should write.

QTR had assured her that before anything was published, they would get her approval. She wouldn't have agreed to the arrangement otherwise. After all, she didn't want them getting the facts wrong.

Although at this point, there wouldn't be much to write about the elusive Mr. Santoro. Giving herself the freedom to write about anything she'd learned so far, she resumed typing.

His estate in in disarray with overgrown vegetation. Was it always this way?

He's run off multiple assistants. What has happened? Has he fired them? If so, for what?

Locked door between the office and the rest of the house. What is he hiding?

The man lacks social niceties. Has he always been this way? Or is this a new thing?

It certainly wasn't a stellar first report. Would they be upset that it contained more questions than answers? Or would they appreciate her train of thought and look forward to the answers?

Accepting that it was the best she could do now, she proofread the email. Gabrielle pressed Send and closed her personal laptop.

She moved to the French doors and stared at the sky—the storm had now moved away. She opened the doors, enjoying the fresh scent of rain in the air. In the distance, the lightning provided a beautiful show. Was Mr. Santoro staring at the sky, too? She instinctively glanced in the direction of the main house, but she couldn't see it as it sat farther back than the guesthouse.

Still, she couldn't stop thinking about her mysterious boss. There had to be a way to break through the man's wall. She would find it, one way or the other.

CHAPTER THREE

Two days…

Forty-eight hours…

Two thousand, eight hundred and eighty minutes…

One hundred seventy-two thousand and eight hundred seconds…

No matter how Gaby stated it, that was how long she'd been at the Santoro estate and how long she'd gone without laying eyes on her new boss. It was weird. Beyond weird. What would that be? Bizarre?

Gaby sighed. Whatever you called it, she wasn't comfortable with this arrangement. Not that her accommodations weren't comfortable. In fact, they were quite luxurious. And unlike the estate's grounds, the guest suite was immaculate, thanks to Mr. Santoro's housekeeper, Mrs. Kupps. The woman had even written her a note, welcoming her.

Gaby glanced at her bedside table and realized that she'd slept in. She only had five minutes until she was due at the office. She had to get a move on. She slipped on a plain black skirt to go with a gray cap-sleeve blouse. There was a jacket that went with the outfit, but she rejected it. It was a warm day and she was more comfortable without the jacket. After all, it wasn't as if she had any business meetings. When Mr. Santoro said that he would limit their interactions to strictly email with the rare phone call, he hadn't been exaggerating.

She stepped in front of the full-length mirror and slipped on her black stilettos. With her height of only five foot two, the extra inches added to her confidence.

A knock sounded at the door, startling Gaby. She knew who it was without even opening the door. It would be Mrs. Kupps trying to lure her into eating breakfast. Gaby already explained that she didn't eat much in the mornings. In all honesty, she loved breakfast but never had time for it. She'd grown used to her liquid diet of coffee, with sugar and milk. It was easy to grab when she was on the run. Upon learning this, Mrs. Kupps had clucked her tongue and told her that she would end up with an ulcer if she didn't take better care of herself.

Gaby rushed to the door. "Good morning."

Mrs. Kupps stood there with a bright smile, a tray full of food and a carafe of coffee. "Good morning to you, too. I just brought you a little something to eat." Mrs. Kupps rushed past her and entered the small kitchen, placing the tray on the bar area. "I know you're in a hurry, but I'm determined to find something you can eat quickly."

"Mrs. Kupps, you don't have to do that." And then, because she really didn't want to hurt the woman's feelings, she added, "But it is really sweet of you. And the food looks amazing."

Mrs. Kupps beamed. "Oh, it's nothing, dearie. I enjoy having someone around here to spoil. Lord knows Mr. Santoro doesn't let anyone fuss over him since the accident. He's like a big old bear with a thorn in his paw."

"So he wasn't always so standoffish?"

Mrs. Kupps began setting out the food. "Goodness, no. He was always gracious and friendly. Perhaps he was a bit wrapped up in his acting career, but that's to be expected with his huge success. But now, he lurks about all alone in that big mansion. He doesn't see guests and rarely takes phone calls. I cook all his favorites, but his appetite isn't what it used to be. I'm really worried about him."

"Do you know what's wrong with him?"

Gaby couldn't help but wonder if the guilt over the accident was gnawing at him.

Mrs. Kupps shrugged. "I don't know. And I really shouldn't have said anything. I just don't want you to leave. We need someone young and spirited around here. Lord knows, we've gone through assistant after assistant. He's even tried to run me off but it's not going to happen." The woman smiled at her. "You're a breath of fresh air. I have a good feeling about you."

Mrs. Kupps checked that everything was as it should be and then made a quick exit. It wasn't until the door shut that Gaby thought of a question for the very kind woman. Why did she stay here? Mr. Santoro was not the easiest person to work for. In fact, he was demanding and expected nothing but perfection with everything that Gaby did. And when she messed up, there was a terse note telling her to fix said error. And he didn't spare the exclamation points.

Still, she had agreed to this arrangement to save her father—a father who was now more eager to know what dirt she had dug up on her boss than worrying about how she was making out in such strained circumstances. It was all he'd wanted to talk about on the phone. His full attention was on making Mr. Santoro pay for the accident.

Gaby's gaze scanned over the croissant and steaming coffee. There was also a dish of strawberries. Okay. So maybe she had enough time to enjoy a few bites. Her stomach rumbled its approval. Perhaps some nourishment would help her deal with the stress of the day.

She couldn't help but wonder if this would be the day that Mr. Santoro revealed himself to her. He couldn't hide from her forever.

Deacon awoke with a jerk. His gaze sought out the clock above the door. He'd slept for more than two hours without waking. That was a new record for him, but it had come at a cost. He'd had another nightmare and, even worse, he was late.

It'd been another night spent in his office. He preferred it to staring into the dark waiting for sleep to claim him. Because with the sleep came the nightmares.

A couple of months after the accident, his nightmares had started to subside. But then Gabrielle's father had staged his protest with a megaphone, and he'd shouted horrible accusations. It was then that the nightmares had resumed. Sometimes Deacon remembered bits and pieces. There were brutal images of fire, blood and carnage. He had to wonder how much was real and how much had been a figment of his imagination.

Other times, he was left with a blank memory but a deep, dark feeling that dogged him throughout the day. It'd gotten so bad that he dreaded falling asleep. That's when his insomnia had set in with a vengeance. After spending one sleepless night after the next, he'd given up sleeping in his bed. In fact, he'd given up on sleep and only dozed when utter exhaustion claimed him.

It'd helped to keep his mind busy. And so he'd become a workaholic. Knowing the movie industry inside and out, he was working on starting his own production business. But being the man behind the curtain meant he had to find people he could rely on to do the legwork for him. That was proving to be a challenging task.

He'd just sat down to read over the lengthy letter that Gabrielle had typed up for him. It had been late in the night or early in the morning, depending on how you looked at it. He'd made it to the last page when his eyes just wouldn't focus anymore. Blinking hadn't helped. Rubbing them hadn't made a difference. And so he'd closed them just for a moment.

He jumped to his feet and gathered up the papers that he'd reviewed. If he didn't get these on Gabrielle's desk before she arrived, it would have to wait until lunchtime. Because the mail drop in the wall only went one way. There was no way for him to deliver any documents anonymously for his assistant. He would have to see about rectifying that, but for now, he had to beat Gabrielle to the office.

He strode toward the door. When he reached out his hand for the doorknob, he couldn't help but notice the webbed scars on the back of his hand. They were a constant reminder of the horror he might have caused that impacted so many lives—especially Gabrielle's.

It was no secret that he'd liked his cars fast and he'd driven them like he was on a racetrack. He couldn't remember the details of that fateful night, but it wouldn't surprise him if he'd been speeding. If only the police would just release their findings. Gabrielle's father wasn't the only one anxious for that report.

His attorney had told him there were a number of complications. There had been an intense fire that destroyed evidence followed by a torrential downpour. Deacon didn't care about any of it. He just needed to know—was he responsible for taking a life?

Deacon moved through the darkened hallway, past the dust-covered statues and the cobwebs lurking in the corners. He didn't care. It wasn't like there was anyone in the house but him. Not even Mrs. Kupps was allowed in this part of the house. She kept to the kitchen and the office suite.

He descended the stairs in rushed steps. When he reached the locked door that led to the office area, he paused. There was no light visible from under the door and no sounds coming from within. He hated sneaking around his own home, but he didn't have any other choice. He didn't want to startle her with his appearance.

He recalled what had happened when his friends, or rather the people he'd considered friends, had visited him in the hospital right after his accident. They were unable to hide their repulsion at seeing the scars on his face, neck and arms. And then he'd held up a mirror to see for himself. The damage was horrific. After numerous rounds of plastic surgery, his plastic surgeon insisted the swelling and red angry scars would fade. Deacon didn't believe him. He'd already witnessed the devastating damage that had been done. It was so bad that he'd removed all the mirrors in the house as well as any reminders of how he used to look.

Deacon banished the troublesome thoughts. What was done, was done. He moved into the office and placed the stack of papers on Gabrielle's desk. That would definitely keep her busy today and probably some of tomorrow.

He noticed that her desk was tidy. However, there were no pictures or anything to tell him a little about her. It was though she wasn't planning to be here one minute longer than necessary to repay her father's debt. Not that Deacon could blame her—no one wanted to be here, including him. But he couldn't go out in the world—not until the accident was resolved and answers were provided.

Without tarrying too long, he turned to leave. He was almost to the door when he heard a key scrape in the lock. For a moment, he wondered what it would be like to linger in the office and have a face-to-face conversation with Gabrielle. In that moment, he realized how much he missed human contact. Maybe if he were to stay—maybe it would be different this time. Maybe she wouldn't look at him like he was a monster—a monster that killed her aunt.

He gave himself a mental shake. It was just a bunch of wishful thinking. He moved with lightning speed to the other door. He grasped the doorknob and, without slowing down, he gave it a yank, slipped into the outer hallway and kept moving. He needed distance from the woman who made him think about how one night—one moment—had ruined things for so many people.

CHAPTER FOUR

DIDN'T THIS MAN SLEEP?

It was almost lunchtime and Gaby hadn't even scratched the surface of all the tasks her boss had left for her. It didn't help that the phone rang constantly. Most calls were from reporters wanting to speak with Deacon. She had been left strict instructions to tell them "no comment" and hang up. With business associates, she was left with explaining that Deacon didn't take phone calls. When she explained that they would have to deal with her, it didn't go over well. Still, Gaby persisted. She had a job to do.

With a sigh, Gaby pressed Send on an email requesting the script for a film that Deacon was considering backing. But from what she could gather from prior correspondence and the files in the office, he had requested a lot of screenplays, but had yet to back one. She wanted to ask him how he decided which would be worth his money and which wouldn't.

Gaby got up to place the mail in the allotted slot for Mr. Santoro. When she approached the mail slot, she noticed the connecting door was slightly ajar. She slipped the papers into the slot and then turned back to the door. It beckoned to her.

What would it hurt to go see what was on the other side?

She knew if Mr. Santoro caught her, he would not be happy. In fact, it could very well blow up their whole deal. But if she didn't take a chance now, would she ever find out what he was hiding?

And to be fair, she was never told that she couldn't enter the house—only that mail was to go in the slot and communication would be phone or email. She had a hard time believing that he was as bad off as Mrs. Kupps had let on. This place wasn't exactly a dungeon by any means. He probably was just avoiding all the unanswered questions about the accident. And it was high time he stopped hiding from the truth and faced up to what had happened.

With a renewed determination, Gaby placed her hand on the doorknob and pulled the door open. It moved easily and soundlessly. There were no lights on in the hallway, but a window toward the back of the house let in some sunshine, lighting her way.

She didn't know what she expected when she crossed the threshold—an enraged Deacon Santoro, or a dark, dank house?—but she found neither. The house was done up in mainly white walls and marble floors. What she did notice was all of the empty spaces on the walls. There were mounted lights as though to illuminate a work of art or a framed photo, but there was nothing below any of the lights, as though even the hangings had been removed. *How odd.* The oddity was beginning to become a theme where Mr. Santoro was concerned.

The first set of doors she came to had frosted-glass inserts. One door stood ajar. She peered inside, wondering if at last she'd come face-to-face with Deacon Santoro, the larger-than-life legend. But the room appeared to be empty—except for all of the books lining the bookshelves.

Her eyes widened as she took in what must be thousands of titles. She stepped farther into the room, finding the bookcases rose up at least two stories. Like a bee to honey, she was drawn to the remarkable library. There was a ladder that glided along a set of rails to reach the top shelves. And a spiral staircase for the second floor of shelves with yet another ladder. It was truly remarkable.

She didn't know whether she had walked onto the set of *My Fair Lady* or the library of *Beauty and the Beast*. She'd never seen anything so magnificent. She moved to the closest bookshelf and found an entire row of leather-bound classics. It was then that she noticed the thick layer of dust and the sunshine illuminating a spiderweb in the corner. Who would neglect such a marvelous place?

Gaby ignored the dust and lifted a volume from the shelf. She opened the cover to find that it was a first edition—a *signed* first edition. It was probably priceless or at least worth more than she could ever pay.

And then she realized that if it was so valuable, she shouldn't be holding it in her bare hands. When she reached out to return it to the shelf, she heard footsteps behind her. She paused, not sure what to do. She moved the book behind her back. The time had come to face Mr. Santoro and suddenly she was assailed with nerves. It probably wouldn't help her case to be found hiding a collector's item. Her hand trembled and she almost dropped the book, but with determination, she gently placed it back on the shelf.

She leveled her shoulders, preparing for a hostile confrontation, and turned. The man had just entered the library and caught sight of her at the same time she had spotted him. He wore jeans and a long-sleeved shirt, which struck her as odd considering it was warm outside. And then she realized he was the man she spotted the first day that she'd arrived. He was the mysterious man from the rose garden.

"Who—who are you?" She didn't take her eyes off him.

His dark eyes narrowed. "I'm the one who should be asking questions here."

The voice, it was familiar. Was it possible that this was Deacon Santoro? She peered closely at him, trying to make up her mind. She supposed that it could be him. But it was his hair that surprised her. It was a longer style, if you could call it a style. The dark strands brushed down over his collar and hung down in his face.

She'd never seen him wear his hair that long in any of the movies he'd played in and yes, she'd seen them all. At one point, she'd have been proud of that fact, but after the accident, she'd wondered what she'd ever seen in the man.

When her gaze returned to his face, she had to tilt her chin upward. He was tall, well north of six feet.

And by the downturn of his mouth, he was not happy to find her in here. Her heart picked up its pace. She should turn away, but she couldn't. She needed to size up the man—all of him. She swallowed hard and jerked her gaze from his mouth. She really had to get a grip on herself. After all, he was the enemy, not some sexy movie star… Okay maybe he was that, too.

Ugh! This is getting complicated.

Her gaze took in the full, thick beard. It covered a large portion of his face. Between the beard and his longer hair, his face was hidden from view, for the most part. Except for his eyes. Those dark mysterious eyes stared directly at her, but they didn't give away a thing.

"What are you doing here?" His voice was deep and vibrated with agitation.

"I was looking for you." She refused to let on that his presence unnerved her. She clasped her hands together to keep from fidgeting. "I thought it was time we met." She stepped forward and held out her hand. "Hello, Mr. Santoro."

His eyebrows drew together and he frowned as he gazed at her hand, but he made no move to shake it. "I told you I don't do face-to-face meetings. And you may call me Deacon."

Gaby recalled what Mrs. Kupps had said about him preferring formality and was surprised he'd suggest she call him by his given name. Perhaps he wasn't as stuck in his ways as she'd originally thought.

"And I don't like to be kept isolated." Ignoring the quiver of her stomach, Gaby withdrew her hand. "If I am going to work with a person, they need to have the decency to meet with me—to talk one-on-one with me."

"You've seen me. Now go!"

She crossed her arms, refusing to budge. It was time someone called him out on his ridiculous behavior. "Does everyone jump when you growl?"

"I don't growl."

She arched a disbelieving eyebrow at him.

"I don't." He averted his gaze.

"You might want to be a little nicer to the people who work for you." And then she decided that pushing him too far would not help her cause, and said, "I have a request that just came in today for you to make an appearance at the upcoming awards show to present an award—"

"No."

"No? As in you don't want to attend? Or no, as in you won't be a presenter?"

"No, as in I'm not leaving this house. And no, I'm not presenting any awards. Have you looked at me? No one would want me in front of a camera."

The fact that he'd dismissed the idea so quickly surprised her. For some reason, she thought he would enjoy being in the spotlight. Isn't that what all movie stars craved?

Deciding it might be best to change the subject, she said, "You have an amazing library."

At first, he didn't say a word. She could feel his gaze following her as she made her way around the room, impressed that the books were placed in the Library of Congress classification system. Was it possible Mr. Santoro... erm, Deacon loved books as much as her?

"I see you have your books cataloged." She turned back to him. "Do you also have a digital catalog?"

He nodded. "The computer that houses the database is over there."

She followed the line of his finger to a small wooden desk next to the door she'd entered. "This place is amazing. I've never known anyone with such an elaborate private library."

His dark eyebrows rose behind his shaggy hair. "You like books?"

"I love them. I'm a librarian and..." Realizing that she was about to reveal that she was an aspiring journalist would only make him more wary of her.

"And what?"

"I was going to say that I read every chance

I get." She turned back to him. "I take it you read, too."

He shrugged. "I used to. These days my reading is all work-related."

"That's a shame, because books are the key to the imagination. You can travel the world between the pages of a book. Or visit another time period. Anything is possible in a book."

"What is your favorite genre?"

"I have two—suspense and romance. And cozy mysteries. And some biographies." She couldn't help but laugh at herself. "I have a lot of favorites. It depends on my mood." Perhaps this conversation was her chance to get past his gruff exterior. "How about you?"

"Mysteries and thrillers." He turned toward the door but paused. Over his shoulder, he said, "You—you may make use of the library while you are here." Then his voice dropped to the gravelly tone. "But do not wander anywhere else. The rest of the house is off-limits."

He certainly growled a lot, but she was beginning to think that his growl was much worse than his bite. So far, so good. Now if she could just get him to open up to her, perhaps she could find the answers to the questions that were torturing her father.

But before she could say another word, Deacon strode out the door.

* * *

Why had he gone and done that?

Later that afternoon, Deacon strode back and forth in his office. He never gave anyone access to the house. Even Mrs. Kupps, who had been with him for years, had restricted access. Now, his house was being overrun by women and he didn't like it.

He'd rather be left alone with his thoughts. His repeated attempts to uncover the truth had been unproductive. He kept coming back to one question: had he been responsible for Gabrielle's aunt's death?

As long as Gabrielle stayed in the library and the office, he could deal with her unwelcome presence. If he wanted a book to distract him from reality, he would make his visits late at night, when he was certain that Gabrielle would be asleep.

The thought of having that beauty staying on the estate gave him a funny sensation in his chest. It wasn't a bad feeling. Instead, it was warm and comforting. Dare he admit it? The sensation was akin to happiness.

It was wrong for him to be excited about Gabrielle's presence. He didn't deserve to be happy. But there was something special about her and it went beyond her beauty. She was daring and fun. He admired the way she stood up to him. He could only imagine that she was just as fiery in bed.

In that moment, his imagination took over. The most alluring images of his assistant came to mind. He envisioned Gabrielle with her long coppery hair splayed over the pillow while a mischievous grin played on her lips. With a crooked finger, she beckoned him to join her.

Eagerness pulsed through his veins as he shifted his stance. He'd been alone so long and she was an absolute knockout. He imagined that she could see past his scars and—

Knock. Knock.

Immediately his lips pulled down into a distinct frown. Who was disturbing his most delicious daydream? Wait. Who was in his private area?

Deacon spun around. Heated words hovered at the back of his mouth. And then his gaze landed on Gabrielle. A smile lifted her glossy red lips. Her eyes were lit up like they had been in his fantasy. He blinked and then peered into her eyes once more. Instead of desire, there was uncertainty.

"What are you doing here?" His words came out much gruffer than he'd planned.

"I—I have some correspondence for you to approve, and I have an idea I want to run by you."

"And for that you marched up here to my private office? You couldn't have emailed me?"

Her lips lowered into a firm line just as her fine eyebrows drew together. "I didn't think you were serious about resuming that ridiculous nonsense of emailing each other. I thought now that you've granted me access to your home, we could start working together like two professionals instead of being pen pals."

His prior assistants never would have been so bold. His respect for Gabrielle grew. And that observation caught him off guard. If he wasn't careful, her tenacity would lead them into trouble. However, she certainly did liven up his otherwise boring existence. Maybe he could risk having his life jostled just a bit.

"Well, you're here now, so out with it. What's your idea?" He had to admit that he was curious.

"I've been thinking over your concern about your public image. And I know that my father didn't help with that. But I've thought of something that might help—"

"Help?" He was utterly confused. "You want to help me?" When she nodded, he asked, "Why?" He was certain there had to be some sort of catch. There was no way she would want to help the person that was involved in an accident that killed her aunt. No one had that good of a heart.

Gabrielle lifted her chin. "During our first phone conversation, you appeared to be upset with the negative publicity, and I've thought of a way to negate some of it."

Some people may call him a pessimist, but the possibility of countering the bad publicity was definitely too good to be true. There was a catch and he intended to find it. "And what's in it for you?"

Her eyes widened. "Why does there have to be more?"

"Because you aren't here out of choice. There is absolutely no reason for you to help me. So out with it. What do you stand to gain?"

She sighed. "Fine. There is something—"

"I knew it." He felt vindicated in knowing that behind that beautiful face was someone with an agenda. "Well, by all means, don't keep me in suspense. What do you want in exchange?"

She frowned at him. "Why do you have to make it sound so nefarious?"

"And why are you avoiding the answer?"

"If my idea works, I was hoping you'd see fit to shorten my time here."

He smiled. "I was right. There is a catch."

"I just think we can help each other is all. Would you consider sponsoring a fundraiser?"

A fundraiser? He had to admit he hadn't seen that coming. "I am the last person who should be asking people for money."

Gabrielle shrugged. "I don't agree. People know who you are. You're up for a couple of awards for your latest movie release. And you have another movie about to be released. I think you'd be surprised by the public's support."

Deacon shook his head. "It's not going to happen."

"Consider it your way to put some good back in the world."

"You mean my penance."

She shrugged and glanced away. "I suppose you could put it that way."

There was no penance big enough, generous enough or selfless enough to undo his actions. "No."

"Because you don't want to do something good?"

Why did she have to keep pushing the subject? He had to say something—anything—to get her to let go of this idea. And then he thought of something that might strike a chord with her. "Have you looked at me?"

"Yes, I have." Her gaze was unwavering.

"Then you know that I have no business being seen in public."

Her gaze narrowed. "I think you're trying to take the easy way out."

"Easy?" His hands clenched. "There is nothing easy about any of this. You of all people should know that."

"You're right. I'm sorry. That didn't come out the way I meant."

He wanted to know what she had meant but he decided the subject was best left alone. "I need to get back to work."

"I think with a haircut and a shave that you'd look…" She stepped closer to him. At last, she uttered softly, "Handsome."

Too bad he didn't believe her. There wasn't a stylish enough haircut to distract people from his scars. And a shave would just make those imperfections obvious. He shook his head. "It isn't going to happen."

"What isn't? The haircut or the shave? Or the fundraiser?"

"All of them." Why couldn't she just leave him alone? It would be better that way.

She crossed her arms and jutted out her chin. "I can do this. And you can participate as much or as little as you want."

"What do you know about fundraisers?"

"Enough. I've organized one for my library each of the past five years."

"A library fundraiser?"

She nodded. "Funds are being withheld from libraries across the country. Lots of them are closing. In order to keep doors open, libraries have become creative in raising money. So many people need and use the resources made available by the library, but the government is of less and less help at keeping the lights on. It's a real struggle."

"I didn't know." It'd been a very long time since he was in a public library. "My mother used to take me to the library when I was very young. I remember they had reading time where all the kids sat around in a circle and they read a story to us. I think that's when I got the acting bug. I'd listen to the librarian use different voices for the various characters and it struck a chord in me."

Gabrielle's smile returned and lit up the room. "As a librarian, that's the best thing I could hear. I love when we are able to make a difference in someone's life, big or small."

"So, what you're saying is that you'd like me to do a fundraiser for your library."

She shook her head. "Not at all. The library is what is close to my heart. You need to find what's closest to yours."

He took a second to think of what charity he'd most like to help and the answer immediately came to him.

"You've thought of something. What is it?" She stared at him expectantly.

"Breast-cancer research. *If* I were going to have a fundraiser, that's what I would want it to be for."

"Why?" she asked, curiosity ringing from her gaze.

He shook his head. He wasn't going to get in to this. Not with her. Not with anyone. It was too painful and still too fresh in his mind.

After a few moments, Gabrielle asked, "Will you at least consider the idea?"

It would be more efficient and less hassle to just write a hefty check, which he did every year in memory of his mother. But Gabrielle seemed to have her heart set on this. Perhaps if he didn't readily dismiss the idea, with time she'd forget about it.

"I'll think about it." When a smile reappeared on her face, he said, "But don't get your hopes up."

She attempted to subdue her smile, but there was still a remnant of it lighting up her eyes as she placed some papers on his desk. Those eyes were captivating. They were gray, or was it green? Honestly, they seemed to change color. And they had gold specks in them. They were simply stunning, just like Gabrielle.

And then as he realized he was staring, Deacon turned away. "I'll get these back to you by morning."

He gazed out the window at the cloudless sky until he heard the clicking of her heels as she walked away. It was then he realized he'd forgotten to tell her something.

He turned around but she was out of sight. He was going to tell her not to enter this part of the house again—that it was out of bounds. But something told him she would have just ignored him anyway.

CHAPTER FIVE

THE NEXT MORNING Deacon couldn't concentrate. He should be working, if he was ever to get his fledgling company firmly ensconced in the movie business. He'd made a lot of inroads so far. The legal documents were all signed and filed with the appropriate agencies. Financial business accounts were opened. Sunsprite Productions was at last ready to do business.

In front of him sat a stack of proposed movie scripts to read. However, every time he sat down, his mind would venture back to Gabrielle. Why had he agreed to keep the door unlocked? To give her access to his space?

He'd avoided the library like the plague and, so far, she hadn't returned to his office. The way she'd looked at him—well, it was different than others. She hadn't shuddered. And she hadn't turned away. If anything, she'd been curious. In fact, she'd even stepped closer to him. What was he to make of that?

No one who'd come to see him in the hospital, people who were supposed to be his friends, had been able to look him in the eye. Most had hovered at the doorway, unwilling to come any closer. But not Gabrielle. She was different. And his curiosity about her kept mounting.

He had to wonder why her aunt had found it necessary to use her last breath to tell him to take care of her niece. He had to be missing something. Gabrielle Dupré was quite capable of taking care of herself.

She hit things straight on and treaded where others feared to go. And she was smart, as she'd demonstrated by coming up with that idea to improve his public image—though he doubted it would work. He needed to tell Gabrielle that he wasn't going to take her up on the offer; he just hadn't gotten around to telling her yet. It wasn't like he had to worry about letting her down. Gabrielle was no damsel in distress. She was sharp and would always land on her feet. Deacon wondered if her father knew how lucky he was to have her by his side.

He halted his train of thought. Listing all of her positive qualities was doing him no favors. No matter how much she intrigued him, nothing could ever come of it.

Because there was a look in her eyes, one that was undeniable. She looked at him with anger. She blamed him for her aunt's death. And for all he knew, she might be right.

Feeling the walls closing in around him, Deacon made his way down to the rose garden. It was the one place where he found some solace. With the gentle scent of the roses that reminded him of his mother and the sea breeze that conjured up memories of sailing, his muscles relaxed. It was here that the pulsing pain in his temples eased.

He moved about the garden. His doctor and physical therapist had told him to make sure to get plenty of movement as that would help heal the injury to his leg caused by the crash. He wasn't about to venture outside the estate gates. He knew the press would soon catch up to him. And then the probing questions would begin.

And so he spent time here in the spacious rose garden. He hadn't spared any expense creating this retreat. The garden ran almost to the edge of the cliff overlooking the ocean. Wanting a wide-open feel, he'd declined building a wall around the garden. He used to think that this garden was a little piece of heaven on earth.

Deacon took a deep breath, enjoying the

fresh air. Out here he could momentarily forget the guilt that dogged him. Out here, he could pretend there wasn't the most amazing yet unobtainable woman working for him. For just a few precious moments, his problems didn't feel so overwhelming.

He followed the meandering brick path to the far edge of the garden. He paused to prune a dying purple rose from a newly planted bush. He'd surprised himself by finding that he didn't mind gardening. In fact, he found the whole process relaxing. Who'd have ever guessed that?

A glint of bright light caught his eye. He glanced around, finding an idle speedboat bobbing in the swells not far off the shoreline. The light must have been a reflection. It wasn't unusual for the water to be filled with boats on these beautiful sunny days. And today, with the brilliant sunrise, it wasn't surprising that people were out enjoying the warm air and the colorful sky.

He didn't give the boat any further attention as he turned back to his task. He continued to trim the dead blooms from the bush when a movement out of the corner of his eye caught his attention. Was it animal? Or human?

Deacon swung around. He didn't see anything. Perhaps it was just his exhaustion catching up to him. With a shake of his head, he returned to his task.

"Good morning."

The sound of Gabrielle's voice startled him. He turned with a jerk. "You shouldn't be here." Did she have to invade every part of his life? Frustration churned within him. "Go!"

Her eyes widened. "I... I'm sorry."

She stepped back. Her foot must have struck the edge of a brick because the next thing he knew, her arms were flailing about and then she was falling. He started toward her, but he was too far away to catch her. And down she went. Straight into a rosebush.

Deacon immediately regretted his harsh words. He didn't mean to scare her. He inwardly groaned as he rushed over to her.

The first thing he spotted was blood. Little droplets of blood dotting her arms and legs from the thorny vines. And it was all his fault. Since when had he become such a growling old bear—so much like the father that he swore he would never turn into. And yet it had happened...

Take care of Gabrielle. There it was again. Her aunt's last dying wish. He was certainly doing a dismal job of it.

As he drew near her, he watched as Gabrielle struggled to sit up. Her movements only succeeded in making the situation worse and a pained moan crossed her lips.

"Don't move," he said, coming to a stop next to her.

This was one of the rosebushes he hadn't gotten to. The limbs were long and unruly. He pulled the shears from his back pocket and hastily cut the bush. He worked diligently to free her.

And then he had her in his arms. Her eyes glistened with unshed tears. She sniffled but she refused to give in to the pain. Her strength impressed Deacon. He was used to women who lashed out or gave in to the tears. Gabrielle was stoic—or perhaps stubborn fit her better.

He started toward the house with her in his arms.

"I can walk," she insisted.

"I've got you."

"Put me down." There was steely strength in her voice and the unshed tears were now gone.

He hesitated, not wanting to put her down. To his detriment, he liked holding her close. She was light and curvy.

And she smelled like strawberries. His gaze lowered to her lips. They were berry-pink and just right for the picking. He forgot about their awkward circumstances and the fact that he hadn't shaved or had a haircut in months.

In that moment, all he wanted to do was pull her closer and press his mouth to hers. Her lips were full and shimmered with lip gloss. It had been so very long since he'd been with a woman—

"Now." Her voice cut through his wayward thoughts.

When his gaze rose up to meet her eyes, she stared up at him with determination. Did she know where his thoughts had drifted? He hoped not. Having her know that he was attracted to her would just make this uncomfortable arrangement unbearable. He lowered her feet to the ground.

"Come with me." This time he was the one issuing orders and he wasn't going to take no for an answer.

He led the way into the darkened house. He knew that in its day the house was impressive, but now the blinds were lowered and dust covered most everything. But it didn't matter to him. He never spent time on the first floor. He stuck to his suite of rooms. And that's where he led Gabrielle.

Into the expansive foyer with its white marble floor and large crystal chandelier. He turned toward the sweeping staircase that curved as it led to the second floor.

"Where are we going?" she asked.

"To get you cleaned and bandaged."

"I'll be fine."

She didn't trust him. That was fine. She had no reason to trust him. He wasn't even sure he trusted himself now that he had a faulty memory and tormenting dreams. But this wasn't about her trusting him. This was about her welfare and making sure she didn't have any serious injuries.

"You need someone to help you." He turned to her at the bottom of the stairs. "You can't reach the cuts on your back. And as fate would have it, today is Mrs. Kupps's day off."

He started up the steps, hoping she would see reason and follow him. The very last thing he needed on his conscience was her being injured because of him and then getting an infection. He may have royally messed up the night of the accident and no matter how much he wanted to go back in time, it was impossible. However, right now he could help Gabrielle. If only she would allow him.

At the top of the steps there were three hallways—one to the left, which was where his mother had had her suite of rooms, another hallway to the right, where the people he'd considered friends used to stay, and then the hallway straight back, which led to his suite of rooms and his office that overlooked the ocean.

He stopped outside the last door. He hadn't made his bed. He hadn't straightened up in forever. And it hadn't mattered to him for months. But now, it mattered. Now he was embarrassed for Gabrielle to see his inner sanctuary. Later tonight he would do some cleaning.

"Is something wrong?" she asked. "If you changed your mind, I can go."

"No. Nothing's wrong." And with that he swung open the door. It wasn't like he was trying to impress her. That ship had sailed a long time ago. In fact, he'd lost any chance to impress her before they'd even met.

The room was dark as the heavy drapes were drawn as they always were, but he knew his way around without bothering with a light. However, he realized that Gabrielle would have a problem, and he reluctantly switched on the overhead light.

"Why is it so dark in here?" she asked. "You should open the curtains and let in the sun."

"I like it this way."

"Maybe the sun would give you a cheerier disposition."

Why did she want to go and change him?

He didn't want to be changed. This was now his life and he would live it however he chose. "My disposition is fine."

"Really? And you think it's normal to go around scowling at people and barking out warnings for them to go away?"

"I do not bark and I do not growl." He turned on the bathroom light.

"Apparently you don't listen to yourself very often."

"You are—" he paused, thinking of the right word to describe her "—you are pushy and…"

"And right about you."

He sighed. "You don't know everything."

"But I do know that you're going to turn down my offer to help you."

He arched an eyebrow and stared at her, finding that she was beautiful even with her hair all mussed up from the rosebush and cuts crisscrossing her arms. It was then that he recognized just how much trouble he was in. There was something about Gabrielle that got under his skin, that made him feel alive again. And made him want to be worthy of her affection.

And if he wasn't careful, he was going to fall for her—head over heels. And that couldn't happen. She would be crazy to fall for him after the car accident. And he didn't deserve to have love in his life—not that he was falling in love with her. He wouldn't let that happen.

But knowing that it was even a possibility had him worried. The best thing he could do for both of their sakes was to keep her around here for as little time as possible. Maybe he should accept Gabrielle's offer to plan the fundraiser. Not that he relished having more attention cast upon him, but he could shorten her time on the estate without arousing her suspicions. She would never know how she got to him.

"What are you smiling about?" Gabrielle was eyeing him suspiciously.

"Who, me? I don't smile. Remember, I growl."

"Oh, I remember. But I saw a distinct smile on your face, so out with it."

What did he have by holding back? He'd strike the deal, set the timetable and soon his life would return to the way it used to be. Why did the thought of his quiet, lonely life no longer sound appealing?

"I accept your offer," he blurted out before he had an opportunity to change his mind.

Her eyes widened. Today, they looked more blue than green. "You do?"

He nodded. "How long do you need?"

"A few months would be ideal."

Months? He was thinking in terms of weeks. "You'll need to do it faster than that."

She thought about it. "How grand do you want to make it?"

"That's up to you."

"Instead of say a grand ball, we could do a garden party."

"That might not be enough of a draw."

"Okay. Give me a little time and I'll come up with some other ideas."

"Just don't take too long. I'd like to do this in the next few weeks."

Her eyes widened. "You don't give a person much room to work, do you?"

"If you're not up to the challenge—"

"I'll do it."

"Good. Now let's get you cleaned up." He led her into the bathroom and set to work cleaning and medicating her injuries.

He felt terrible that she'd been injured because of him. He would work harder in the future not to be so abrasive. He'd obviously been spending too much time alone.

He stood in front of her as she sat on the black granite countertop. He'd just used a cloth to wash the wounds on her arms with soap and water. Now that they were rinsed off, he was gently patting them dry.

As he stood there, he could sense her staring at him. He glanced up to say something, but when his gaze caught hers, he hesitated. And then her gaze lowered. Was she staring at his lips?

CHAPTER SIX

WAS THAT DESIRE reflected in her eyes?

Deacon swallowed hard. Suddenly the walls seemed to close in around them and the temperature was rising…quickly. He should turn away because if she kept staring at him, he was going to start to think that she wanted him—almost as much as he wanted her.

"You shouldn't do that," he said.

"Do what?" Her voice carried a note of innocence.

He inwardly groaned. "You know what."

"If I did, I wouldn't ask."

Surely she couldn't be that naive. Could she? "Look at me like—like you want me to kiss you."

She didn't blush, nor did she look away. "Is that what you think I want? Or is that what you want?"

Why did she have to insist on confusing matters? He was already confused enough for both of them. "Forget I said anything."

"How am I supposed to do that now that I know you're thinking about kissing me?"

"That's not what I said." He huffed in exasperation. "Turn around."

"Why?"

"Do you have to question everything?"

She shrugged. "If I didn't, I wouldn't know that you want to kiss me."

"Would you quit saying that?" Heat rushed up his neck and settled in his face, making him quite uncomfortable. "Turn around so I can tend to the wounds on your back."

For once, she did as he said without any questions. Thank goodness. He wasn't sure how much longer he could have put up with the endless questions. It would have been so much easier to smother her lips with his own. And then he'd know if her berry-red lips were as sweet as they appeared.

But this was better. With her back to him, he could get a hold on his rising desire. They were oh, so wrong for each other. She was pushy and demanding. She was definitely not the type of woman he normally dated. If he hadn't been alone all these months, he wouldn't even be tempted by her. He assured himself that was the truth.

And then she lifted her shirt, stained with thin traces of blood, to reveal the smooth skin of her back. His assurances instantly melted away. All he wanted to do was run his hands over her body and soothe away her discomfort with his lips, fingers and body.

"Is something the matter?" she asked.

His mouth suddenly grew dry. He swallowed and hoped when he spoke that his voice didn't give away his wayward thoughts. "I—I'm just figuring out where to start."

"Is it that bad?"

He wondered if she was referring to his level of distraction or the cuts and punctures on her back. He decided that she'd given up flirting with him and was at last being serious. "It could be worse."

"That's not very positive."

He was beginning to wonder if along with his memory loss he'd lost his ability to talk to women. He used to be able to flirt with the best of them without even breaking a sweat, but talking to Gabrielle had him on edge, always worrying that he'd say something wrong, which he seemed to do often.

"I didn't mean to worry you." He grabbed a fresh washcloth from the cabinet and soaked it with warm water. He added some soap and worked it into a lather. "Let me know if this hurts."

"It'll be fine."

He wanted to say that the skin on her back was more tender than that on her arms or hands, but he didn't want to argue with her. It was then that he noticed how her skirt rode up her legs, giving a generous view of her thighs. His hand instinctively tightened around the washcloth as his body tensed.

With great reluctance, he glanced away. It took all of his effort to concentrate on the task at hand. And it didn't help that the task involved running his fingers over her bare flesh. Talk about sweet torture.

He pressed the cloth gently to the first wound. When he heard the swift intake of her breath, he pulled away the cloth. "I'm sorry."

"It's okay. Just keep going."

"Are you sure?"

"Keep going. I obviously can't do it myself."

And so he kept working as quickly as he could. When her wounds were cleaned, rinsed and dried, he grabbed the antibiotic cream, which, thankfully, had something for pain relief. A few of the cuts had required bandages. The others had already started the healing process.

He lowered her top. "There. All done."

She turned to him. "Thank you."

"Don't." He waved off her gratitude. "I don't deserve your thanks."

"Yes, you do. You fixed me all up."

"I'm the one who caused your injuries." He just couldn't seem to do anything right these days.

"No, you didn't. I stumbled and fell. End of story."

"You stumbled because I startled you."

Her green-gray eyes studied him for a moment. "You do have a way of growling—"

His voice lowered. "I don't growl."

She laughed. "You just growled at me."

Had he growled? No, of course not. He wasn't some sort of animal. He was human—a damaged human, but human nonetheless. Still, his tone might have been a bit gruff.

She stepped toward him. "I see the doubt in your eyes."

He narrowed his gaze on her. "If I growl so much, why are you still here?"

"Good question. I guess I'm just holding up my side of our agreement."

For a moment there, he'd forgotten that she was there at his insistence. He knew that if she had a chance, she'd be anywhere else. And he couldn't blame her. He definitely wasn't the most hospitable host.

But when he was this close to Gabrielle, he wanted to be someone else. His old self? No. He'd been too selfish—too self-absorbed. Right now, he wanted to be someone better.

"I'm sorry that I startled you earlier." He made sure when he spoke that his voice was soft and gentle. He would not growl at her. "I never meant for you to get hurt."

She stared into his eyes. "You really mean that, don't you?"

"Of course." His voice took on a rough edge again. He swallowed hard. And when he spoke, he made sure to return to a gentle tone. "I'm not used to having anyone out in the gardens."

"The rose garden is beautiful. That's why I was out there. I could see them from my bedroom window and I wanted to get a better look. Unlike the rest of the grounds, they are well-maintained. They must be special to you?"

"They are. I had them planted for my mother." He missed his mother. She had been kind and gentle. She had been the exact opposite of his brutal father. "Roses were her favorite. She used to spend hours out there. It's where she spent her last days."

Gabrielle's eyes filled with sympathy. She reached out to him. Her fingers wrapped around his hand. She gave him a squeeze. "I know that saying I'm sorry isn't enough, but it's all I have."

He continued to stare into her eyes, and he saw something more than sympathy. There was…understanding. He searched his memory and he recalled her mentioning that she'd also lost her mother. "You understand?"

She nodded. "My mother died giving birth to me, so I never knew her."

Instead of offering her the same empty words, he nodded and squeezed her hand back. It was then he realized her hand was still in his. The physical contact sent a bolt of awareness through his body.

He should let her go. He should step away. But he could do neither of those things. It was as though she were a life-sustaining force and without her, he would cease to exist.

His gaze lowered to her lips. Today they were done up in a striking purple shade. Against her light skin, her lips stood out. They begged for attention and he couldn't turn away.

This wasn't good—not for his common sense. Because right now, all he could think about was her mouth—her very inviting mouth. He wanted to kiss her. He needed to kiss her. He longed to feel those lush purple lips move beneath his. A groan swelled in the back of his throat, but he choked it back down. He didn't need Gabrielle realizing how much power she had over him.

Because there was no way her kiss could be as amazing as he was imagining. Nothing could be that good. Not a chance.

He needed a heavy dose of reality to get her out of his system. And then he'd be able to think clearly. Yes, that would fix things.

Without giving his actions further thought, he dipped his head. He captured her lips with his own. At first, he heard the swift intake of her breath. She pulled back slightly and he thought she was going to turn away.

Then her hand lifted and smoothed over his beard. It must have caught her off guard. He should shave it, but it never seemed like the right time, until now.

And then her lips were touching his again. Tentatively at first. She didn't seem to know what to make of this unlikely situation. That made two of them, because kissing her was the absolute last thing he thought he'd be doing this morning.

As if he were acting in a trance, he drew Gabrielle closer and closer. He expected her to pull away. To slap him. Or at the very least stomp away.

Instead her hands came to rest on his chest. Her lips began moving beneath his. Her hands slid up over his shoulders and wrapped around his neck as her soft curves leaned against him. Mmm…she felt so good. And she tasted sugar-sweet, like the icing on a donut. And he couldn't get enough of her.

Their kiss escalated with wild abandon. It was as if she were the first woman to ever kiss him. No one had stirred him quite the way she did. He never wanted to let her go.

In the background, there was a noise. He couldn't make it out. And then it stopped. Their kiss continued as his body throbbed with need.

And then the sound started again. He wanted it to stop—for them to be left alone to enjoy this very special moment. The next thing he knew, Gabrielle braced her hands against his chest and pulled back.

It was too soon. He wasn't ready to let her go. And yet she moved out of his embrace. She reached for her cell phone, which was resting on the countertop.

"Hello, Dad. Is something wrong?" She turned her back to Deacon.

He ran the back of his hand over his lips. Instead of getting Gabrielle out of his system, he only wanted her more. He was in so much trouble.

Gabrielle turned back to him. She didn't have to tell him how much she loved her father. It was there in her voice when she spoke of him. It was in her eyes. It was in her actions by coming here and working for Deacon. She was a devoted daughter. Deacon just hoped her father deserved such devotion.

When she ended the call, Deacon asked, "Is everything all right with your father?"

She nodded her head. "He's fine."

Deacon noticed how her gaze failed to meet his. "But he's not happy about you being here."

"No. He isn't." She sighed. "My father used to be such an easygoing guy. But the accident, well, it changed everything—for both of us."

Right then the wall went back up between them. Deacon could feel the warmth slip away. The chill was as distinct and real as the kiss they'd shared—the kiss that would not be followed by another. He would be left with nothing more than the memory.

"I know how death can change people." His mother changed after his father's death. Even though the man didn't deserve her undying love, she'd given it to him anyway. When his father passed away, his mother was cloaked in sadness. She moved on with her life, but it was never the same. She was never the same again.

Gabrielle's gaze briefly met his. "About what happened between us—"

"It was nothing." He was a liar. A bold-faced liar. "We lost our heads for a moment. It won't happen again." At least that part was the truth.

Gabrielle glanced away. "You're right. It was a mistake."

Her sharp words stabbed at him. He didn't

know how much more of this he could take. It was best that they parted ways until he got his emotions under control.

He wasn't mad at her. He was angry with himself for losing control—for complicating an already messy situation.

"I should go." She just turned and walked away.

This situation was such a mess. An awful mess. How in such a short time had Gabrielle taken his dark hopeless life and filled it with light? He didn't know how he'd go back to the dark again.

CHAPTER SEVEN

THE SUN WAS sinking into the sky when Gaby called it quits for the day. Deacon had made himself scarce the rest of the day and perhaps that was for the best—for both of them.

Things were confusing enough. That kiss only intensified the conflicting emotions within her. She had no business flirting with him—coaxing him into kissing her. She should keep a respectable distance from this man. He was trouble.

Wait. Was that the answer? Could she be drawn to Deacon because he was so different from the other professional men she'd dated? Did Deacon's dark side act like a magnet?

Whatever it was, she had to get a grip on it. Because her reason for being here had absolutely nothing to do with becoming romantically involved with Deacon Santoro. And she'd do well to remember the circumstances that had led her here.

Gaby sighed as she let herself inside the guesthouse. There was still enough light filtering in from outside that she didn't turn on the lights. Instead she kicked off her heels and moved to the couch.

Her cell phone rang. She didn't recognize the number. She was about to ignore it when she thought of her father. Something might have happened to him.

Needing to be certain her father was all right, she answered the call. "Hello."

"Gabrielle Dupré?" The male voice was unfamiliar to her.

Concern pumped through her veins. "Yes."

"My name's Paul. I'm with *Gotcha* magazine. Do you have a comment on the photo?"

"Photo?" She had no idea what this man was talking about. Thinking it was probably a scam, her finger hovered over the end button.

"The one of you in Deacon Santoro's arms. Would you like to comment on why you're in the arms of the man that *allegedly* killed your aunt?"

"There is no photo."

"If you don't believe me, go to our website. It's on the home page, front and center. I'll wait," he said smugly.

Gaby pressed the end button. It didn't matter what they had posted on their website, she wasn't giving a comment. But she wanted to see what had prompted the reporter to call her.

Her fingers moved rapidly over the touch screen and then the website popped up. She gasped. It was true. They did have a photo of her and Deacon.

Her face felt as though it was on fire. That man had made the situation sound so scandalous. Deacon had only been helping her after she'd been an utter klutz.

She studied the photo more intently. She didn't recall Deacon looking at her like—like he desired her. Surely they'd done something to alter the photo. She'd heard they do that all the time to make people thinner or prettier.

Thankfully there hadn't been any cameras in Deacon's house. Her face burned with embarrassment when she recalled how she'd flirted with him and then that kiss—oh, that heated kiss had been so good.

And yet, the kiss could not be repeated.

No matter how good it was, it was a one-time thing—a spur-of-the-moment thing. It didn't matter if his touch had been so gentle and so arousing. There could be no future for them. It was impossible. She was the niece of the woman who'd died because of Deacon's actions. There was no way they could get around that.

And she wouldn't do that to her father. She

owed everything to her father—a man who'd always stood by her and who'd encouraged her to follow her love of books and sacrificed so that she could go to college.

She needed to talk to Deacon. She needed to tell him about the photo. She headed out the door. She also needed to make sure he'd heard her when she said that she regretted that soul-stirring, toe-curling kiss—because she did, didn't she?

Now that she had full access to the house, she knew her way around. She knew where Deacon would be, where he spent most of his time—in his office. It was like a one-room apartment. From what she could tell, it was where he took his meals, where he slept—when he slept—and where he worked.

Her footsteps were silent over the carpeting. When she reached his office, the door was open and the soft glow of the desk lamp spilled out into the hallway. But there were no sounds inside.

She stepped just inside the door. Her gaze scanned the room, with its long shadows. The desk chair was empty and so was the leather couch. Her gaze continued around the room until she spotted him standing in the open French doors that overlooked the ocean.

He didn't move. He must be lost in thought.

She wondered if she was too late. Had he seen the photo?

She softly called out, "Deacon."

He didn't turn to her as she'd expected. Instead he said, "You shouldn't be here."

"We need to talk."

"If it's business, it can wait."

She crossed her arms and leveled her shoulders. "If you're going to talk to me, you could at least have the decency to face me."

He turned to her. His face was devoid of expression. She didn't know how he managed that when she was certain he was anything but calm—not after that spine-tingling kiss. She supposed that was what made him such an accomplished actor. She, on the other hand, wore her emotions on her sleeve. She didn't like it, but she didn't know how to hide her emotions.

"I'm facing you," he said matter-of-factly. "Now, why are you here?"

"I just had a phone call from a reporter. There's a photo of us on the internet."

A muscle in Deacon's jaw twitched. "Let me see it."

Recalling how the photo made it seem like there was something going on between them, she didn't think Deacon would take it well. "I don't think you want to see it."

He approached her and held out his hand.

She pulled up the picture on her phone. The headline read: Evading the Police in the Arms of a New Lover. Maybe bringing it to Deacon's attention wasn't a good idea after all.

She handed him the phone and waited for his reaction.

For a moment, he didn't speak. He scrolled through the article. With a scowl on his handsome face, he returned her phone.

"I don't even know how they got the photo," she said.

"I do. There was a boat not far off the shoreline. I hadn't thought much of it at the time, but there must have been a photographer on board."

"How can they publish this stuff? The headline is a lie."

"Welcome to my world. The tabloids will do anything for headlines. They are vultures."

"But they know it's not true."

"They don't care about the truth. It's whatever makes them money. I'm sorry you got caught up in it." He raked his fingers through his hair. "Until the police report is released, I'll be in the headlines."

They'd both been dancing around the subject of the car accident for far too long now. She needed some answers and she didn't know how to get them other than being direct. "Deacon, tell me about the accident."

"No." He moved to his desk and started moving papers as though he were looking for something.

"Don't dismiss me. I need to know—I need to know if what my father is saying about you is true."

Deacon straightened and his dark gaze met hers. "Why would you doubt him?"

"Because I feel like I'm missing something. And yet I keep thinking if you were innocent, you would have given your statement to the police. You would have cleared up this mess. Instead you remain tight-lipped about the facts, which says you're guilty. Is that it? Are you guilty?"

His jaw tightened. "I know in part you agreed to this arrangement to get information, but I'm not talking about the accident. Not now. Not ever. So if that's what you're after, you can go back to Bakersfield."

"So you can say I broke the arrangement and have you press charges against my father? No thank you. I'm staying until my time has been served."

"This isn't a prison." His voice rumbled. "You're free to go."

"When our deal is fulfilled and not a minute sooner."

She paused and studied his face. "You might feel better if you talked about it."

"That subject is off-limits," he said with finality.

She sighed. "Okay then. I'll go work on the plans for the fundraiser. I'll let you know how it goes."

"At this hour?"

"It's not like I have much else to do around here. This place is so big and yet so empty."

His eyes grew dark. "It's the way I like it."

She didn't believe him. He didn't live alone in this big house because he wanted to. There was so much more to him closing himself off from the outside world. How would she get him to open up to her?

Gaby moved to the door. She paused in the doorway. She still hadn't told him the other reason she'd sought him out. She worried her lip. With him standing there looking so cold, it wasn't easy to talk to him. He reminded her of the man she'd met that not-so-long-ago day in the library, but tonight he hadn't told her to get out. Nor had he growled at her. Maybe he was changing.

"What?" he prompted.

"I just wanted to make sure that things

were straight between us. You know, about the kiss."

He brushed off her concern. "It's already forgotten. I won't be kissing you again if that's what you're worried about."

"Oh." She wasn't sure what she'd wanted him to say, but that wasn't it.

Without a word, he turned his back to her and stared out at the moon-drenched ocean.

She had been dismissed, quickly and without hesitation. And so had their kiss. Was it just her that had been moved when his lips touched hers?

As she walked away, she felt as though she had lost her footing with Deacon. Her fingers traced her lips, recalling the way his mouth had moved passionately over hers, bringing every nerve ending to life. Her lips tingled at the memory.

He may deny it, but he'd felt something, too. And for the life of her, she didn't know what to do about this attraction that was growing between them.

CHAPTER EIGHT

HE COULDN'T STOP thinking about that picture.

The next morning, Deacon set aside his pen and leaned back in his desk chair. Although he didn't like the invasion of privacy, that wasn't what was eating at him. Nor was it the inflammatory headline. It wasn't any of that stuff.

He pulled up the photo on his computer with the larger monitor. The part that he couldn't get past was that she looked good in his arms. In fact, if he didn't know better, he'd swear they were lovers. And he was certain that's what anyone who caught a glimpse of the photo would think.

He scrolled down, finding there were hundreds of comments. He knew he shouldn't read them, but he couldn't help himself. There were, of course, mean, nasty comments, but to his surprise, there were others in support of them. They commented that sometimes love comes at the most unexpected times. Those people were all wrong—very wrong. Others said he was taking advantage of Gabrielle. That, too, was untrue. He was trying to help her, both financially, with an inflated salary, and so that she could gain her independence from her father. And it certainly had nothing whatsoever to do with love.

Deacon shut down the site. He'd read enough. He checked the time. It was almost time for him to leave for his appointment.

He moved to his bedroom to change clothes. Still, he couldn't stop thinking about Gabrielle.

He knew she wanted answers, but he didn't think she'd buy his amnesia story any more than the police had bought it. There had been the skeptical looks followed by the prodding questions that went on and on with the same answers. It was as if they believed that if they asked the same questions a hundred and one times, his answers would change from "I don't remember" to something they could use against him.

In the short amount of time he'd spent with Gabrielle, he'd come to respect her. And having her upset with him for not opening up about the deadly accident was better than the look she would give him upon hearing that he couldn't remember it. In her shoes, he probably wouldn't believe him, either. He couldn't bear to have her look at him as if he were a liar. He was a lot of things in life, and some of them were not so good, but he wasn't a liar.

Maybe today he would get those elusive answers. His attorney had said he had news, but he wouldn't say on the phone whether it was good or bad. Something told Deacon that it wasn't good news. But he didn't want to say anything to Gabrielle until after his meeting, when he'd hopefully have more information.

Once he left the attorney's office, he had a doctor's appointment, where they'd run some tests to make sure he was healing properly. The accident had done significant damage to his body. If he were to pass through the metal detectors at the airport, he'd surely set them off with his newly acquired hardware.

In the end, he'd spend most of the day in Los Angeles. He didn't like these outings. They were fraught with the stress of being hounded by the press and wondering if the attorney and doctors would have more bad news for him.

Refusing to dwell on the unknowns awaiting him, he gathered the screenplay he'd finished reading. He was on the fence about this one. It was a mystery and he recalled Gabrielle mentioning that she enjoyed reading mysteries. He'd like to get her take on this one before he went any further. He did have a few changes he'd like to see incorporated when the screenplay was rewritten, but he'd run those past Gabrielle after he got her initial reaction.

However, when he opened the door to the office, Gabrielle wasn't at her desk. He walked farther into the room and found the outer door slightly ajar. He dropped the stack of papers on her desk and headed out the door. Once outside, he spotted Gabrielle at the end of the walk.

Deacon called out to her, but she must not have heard him as she kept moving. She turned the corner away from the beach and the guest cottage. Where was she going?

As he followed her, the sidewalk soon became surrounded by overgrown bushes, tall grass and weeds. He frowned. To be honest, he never walked toward the front of the house. It was too close to the road for his comfort with the paparazzi lurking about.

Surely she couldn't be enjoying a leisurely stroll through this thick vegetation, could she? He kept walking. His steps were long and quick as he hustled to catch up with her.

He turned a corner and there she was on the opposite side of the house. She stood in the shadows with a legal pad in one hand and a pen in the other. She was so intent on writing something that she didn't appear to notice his presence.

Once he was within a few yards of her, he called out to her.

Her head jerked up.

"Oh. It's you." And then she flashed him a smile that filled his insides with warmth. "Good morning."

"I stopped down to speak with you and didn't find you at your desk."

She turned back to the legal pad and continued writing. "I had an idea and I needed to check it out. Now, I'm not sure how to make it work."

An idea? Suddenly he grew uncomfortable. If he knew anything about Gabrielle, it was that she wasn't afraid to shake things up. And the fact that she was standing in his overgrown yard making notes didn't sit well with him.

She sent him a mischievous grin that lit up her eyes and intensified that fuzzy warm feeling in his chest. He swallowed hard. "Gabrielle, dare I ask what you have in mind?"

She glanced around. "This used to be a golf course, didn't it?"

He glanced over the neglected grounds and a fresh wave of guilt washed over him. "At one point, it was a private course."

"Wow." Her gaze was glued to the lush green grounds. "How many holes?"

"Nine." He used to spend a lot of time out here entertaining friends and associates. They said he had the best private course in the country. "But it doesn't matter anymore."

"Of course it matters. Why don't you golf anymore?"

"After the accident, my injuries made it impossible."

"And now, can you play?"

"I don't know. I haven't tried." He rotated his left shoulder. There was a dull pain, but thanks to lots of therapy, his range of motion was almost one-hundred-percent. "Not that anyone could golf out here."

"It looks like at one point it was beautiful."

"It was." His mind conjured up an image of the golf course in its prime. It had come with the house and it had been gorgeous, with water hazards and sand bunkers. It might have been a short course, but it had been a fun way to while away a lazy summer afternoon with friends. Those carefree days seemed like a lifetime ago now.

"It's a shame to let it go to ruin. Have you ever considered restoring it?"

He shook his head. He just couldn't imagine golfing when he had so much uncertainty and guilt weighing him down. "I stopped by to let you know that I need to go out for a while."

Her eyes widened and her mouth gaped open, but she quickly recovered her composure. "I didn't know you ever left here."

"I don't unless it's necessary."

Unasked questions filled her eyes, but she was smart enough to leave them unspoken. "Is there anything you need from me while you're gone?"

"Yes. I put a screenplay on your desk. I know you enjoy mysteries and I was interested in your thoughts. The sooner, the better."

"Thoughts? As in a pro-con list?"

He hadn't thought of that, but it wasn't a bad idea. "Sure. That works for me." And then he added, "I'd really appreciate it."

"Well, when you put it so nicely, I'd be happy to do it."

So nicely? He didn't think he'd said it in any special manner. Perhaps she meant since he didn't growl at her. Was Gabrielle having that much of an effect on him?

"I'll be gone most of the day." He turned to walk away.

"Do you mind if I ask where you're going?" When he turned back to her, she added, "You know, in case something comes up while you're gone."

"I'll have my cell phone. The number is listed on your computer."

"Oh, okay." She tried to hide it, but he caught the hint of a frown. "But there's something I want to discuss with you."

He checked the time on his phone. "It'll have to wait."

When he turned to walk away, Gabrielle said, "But it won't take long—"

"I can't be late. I'll talk to you when I get back."

Without another word from either of them, he strode away. He could have told her about his meeting with his attorney, but he didn't want to get her hopes up. He felt the pressure every time she looked at him. She wanted the truth as much as he did. If only he could remember.

This was pointless.

Gaby sat behind her desk later that afternoon. Deacon still hadn't returned. The fact that he'd been gone for hours worried her. Perhaps she should have pushed harder to learn his destination, but she doubted there was anything she could say to get him to open up.

She was quickly coming to the conclusion that no matter what she tried, Deacon wasn't going to let his guard down with her. He was a very determined man. But at least he didn't growl at her any longer. That had to mean something, right?

And now that she had him considering the fundraiser, she had to make it extra special. It was her ticket out of here without jeopardizing the deal for her father.

The fundraiser needed to be something different. Something that would attract big names with big money and also attract the press. She told herself that concluding their deal early was the only reason she was so invested in these plans that kept her up at night. Because there was no way she was trying to improve Deacon's image.

Her gaze scanned across the manuscript that Deacon wanted her to read. It could wait until later. Right now, she was wound up about the fundraiser. It could help so many people, not just Deacon.

After making some notes, Gaby looked up the name and number of the printing company she'd used for the library fundraiser. Lucky for her, she could use a lot of the same contacts for this event. It would cut down on her workload because getting this estate ready for the event was going to take a lot of time.

Gaby recalled seeing a list of estate employees on her first day here when she'd been checking out everything. Now where had she seen it? Her gaze scanned her desktop. Nothing there. Then she turned to the bulletin board behind her desk. No names and numbers.

She logged on to her computer. Maybe they were in here. A lot of pertinent information was stored on the network. She clicked on directory after directory. And then she stumbled across a file titled Personnel Listing. Under Grounds Crew, there were six names listed. Was it possible they were still employees? She knew it was a long shot, but hope swelled within her.

She reached for the phone and then hesitated. Should she do this without checking with Deacon?

She worried her bottom lip. He did give her the lead on this fundraiser. And it wasn't like he had much interest in the plans. But if she could show him what she had in mind, she was certain he would agree. She hoped.

Without letting any more doubts creep into her mind, she picked up the phone and dialed the first number on the list.

CHAPTER NINE

IT HAD NOT been a good day.

Not at all.

Deacon stepped out of the dark SUV and sent the door flying shut with a resounding thud. He pulled the baseball cap from his head, scrunched it with his hand and stuffed it in his back pocket. He removed his dark sunglasses and hung them from the collar of his shirt. He was done with disguises for today.

For all of the good it had done him, he might as well have stayed home. His attorney didn't have any good news for him. In fact, it was quite the opposite. The television network he'd been negotiating with had pulled out of the deal. They felt he brought too much bad publicity to the table and it would ruin their chances of having a hit. Apparently they didn't subscribe to the notion that there is no such thing as bad publicity.

Perhaps Gabrielle was right. Maybe he

needed an image makeover. But would that work before the police report was released?

People might think that he'd refused to answer the officer's questions, but it was quite the opposite. In fact, at his meeting with his attorney, he told him in no uncertain terms to light a match under the powers that be. If he was innocent, he needed to be cleared ASAP. And if he had caused the tragedy, then he'd deal with the consequences.

When he'd moved on to his doctor's appointment, he grilled his physician about the gaping holes in his memory and the nightmares that plagued him. The doctor said the memories might all come back to him at once, or they might come back in pieces. His dreams were indicative of them coming back to him bit by bit. The doctor did warn him that the dreams might be real memories or they could be figments of his imagination. Or a combination of both.

When Deacon stepped out of the garage, he ran straight in to Gabrielle. He was not in the mood to be social right now. "What are you doing here? Shouldn't you be working?"

Her eyes widened. "I am going up to my rooms. And no, I shouldn't be working as the workday is over."

He pulled out his phone. It was much later

than he'd been expecting. His appointments had taken up his entire day and he still didn't know any more than he had when he'd left that morning.

"I—I didn't realize the time." Not wanting to chitchat, he said, "I'll just be going."

"Wait. I wanted to talk to you."

"About?"

"The fundraiser. I've come up with some really good ideas. I was hoping for your input."

Deacon shook his head. He was in no frame of mind to deal with Gabrielle or the fundraiser. "I don't think this evening is a good idea."

"Are you feeling all right?"

"As good as can be expected. I just…" He paused as he grasped for any excuse to make a quick exit. "I'm just hungry."

"Then I have the perfect solution. It's Mrs. Kupps's night off, so I'll cook us up some dinner."

"I don't want you to go to any bother."

"It's no bother. We both have to eat, don't we?"

Her insistence surprised him. Of course, he realized that her interest was purely for business reasons. And she was right, they did have to eat. So what would it hurt to combine food and work?

"Okay. Count me in." He arched an eyebrow at her. "I take it this means you know how to cook."

She nodded. "Does that surprise you?"

"It's just that I don't know much about you."

"What would you like to know?"

A bunch of questions sprang to mind, like was she seeing anyone? If circumstances were different, would she go out with him? He immediately squelched those inquiries. They were none of his business—no matter how much he longed to know the answers.

He swallowed hard. "How well do you cook?"

A smile lifted her pink lips. "Don't you think you should have asked before agreeing to this meal? Now you'll just have to find out for yourself. Come on."

She didn't even wait for his reply before she started up the steps to the guesthouse. He watched the gentle sway of her hips as she mounted each step. No one had a right to look that good. And oh, boy, did she look good.

He hesitated. Right now, he was truly regretting agreeing to this meal. And it had absolutely nothing to do with his bad day or his uncertainty about her cooking skills and everything to do with how appealing he found the cook.

She glanced over her shoulder. "Well, come on."

Not wanting her to notice his discomfort, he did as she said. He started up the steps right behind her. A meal for two. This was a mistake. And yet he kept putting one foot in front of the other.

He'd spent so much time alone that he wasn't even sure he remembered how to make small talk. Just stick to business. It wasn't like she wanted to have this dinner for them to get closer. She was just anxious to get on with this fundraiser—a fundraiser that he was certain would fail if it had his name attached to it.

What had she done?

Gabrielle entered the galley kitchen. It was small and cozy. If Deacon were to be in here with her, they'd be all over each other—as in bumping in to each other. But now that the seed had been planted, she started to think of other things they could cook up together that had absolutely nothing to do with food.

Her imagination conjured up a shirtless Deacon in her kitchen. Oh, yes, things would definitely heat up. And then she'd be there in him arms. Her hands would run over his muscled chest. And there was a can of whipped cream—

Heat rushed to Gaby's face. This was a mistake.

But as she heard Deacon's footsteps behind her, she knew that it was too late to change her mind. She just had to keep her attention focused on the main course and not the dessert.

She moved to the fridge and pulled the door open. There on the top shelf sat the whipped cream. She ignored it. "What are you hungry for?" She was hungry for... The image of licking cream off Deacon came to mind. She gave herself a mental jerk. "Maybe I, ah, should tell you what I have ingredients for and, um, then we can go from there."

"Are you okay?"

"Um, sure." If only she could get the image of having him for dessert out of her mind. "Why?"

"You're acting nervous. If it's dinner, don't worry. We can order in."

"No." Her pride refused to give up. "I've got this."

Deacon took a seat at the kitchen counter. "I'm not a picky eater. So anything is good."

"Let me see what's in here." Mrs. Kupps had kindly offered to fill her fridge for the times when she was off and for the evenings when Gabrielle might get hungry.

"I've found a steak." Gaby opened the produce drawer. "There are some fingerling potatoes. And some tomatoes, onions, Gorgonzola cheese and arugula."

Her gaze skimmed back over that tempting whipped cream, but she absolutely refused to mention dessert. When he didn't respond, she glanced over her shoulder. "What do you think?"

"Sounds good. I'll just look over this information about the fundraiser while you cook the food."

She closed the fridge and turned to him. "I don't think so."

His dark eyebrows drew together as his puzzled gaze met hers. "What?"

"I'm not cooking us dinner. We're both doing it."

He shook his head and waved off her idea. "That is not a good idea. I don't know my way around a kitchen. That's what takeout menus are for."

"It's about time you learned your way around it." She wasn't about to wait on him. She didn't care how much money he had or how famous he was. "Come on. You can wash the potatoes and get them ready to go in the oven while I get out the ingredients for the salad."

And so with a heavy sigh, he got off the bar stool and made his way into the kitchen. She gave him detailed instructions and they set to work. This wasn't as bad as she'd been imagining.

Gabrielle finished rinsing the lettuce and turned to grab a bowl from one of the cabinets over the counter when she ran in to Deacon. To steady herself, she reached out with both hands. They landed on his chest—his very firm chest. The breath caught in her throat.

He reached out, catching her by the waist. His hands seemed to fit perfectly around her. It was though they fit together. But how could that be?

Deacon was the man who was responsible for her aunt's death. At least that's what her father and the papers were saying. But there was a voice deep inside her that said there was so much more to this man. Was she only seeing what she wanted to see?

Neither of them moved as her gaze rose from his chest to his full beard to his straight nose. And then she noticed his hair. It looked like it hadn't been cut in months. It fell just above his eyes. When their gazes at last connected, her heart pounded. Each heartbeat echoed in her ears.

Was it wrong that she wanted him to kiss her again? That kiss they'd shared was stuck in her mind. No man had ever made her feel so alive with just a kiss. And she hadn't gotten enough. Maybe it was the knowledge that it was wrong that made this thing—whatever you wanted to call it—between them that much more enticing. Deacon was the bad boy and she was the good girl.

Her gaze slipped back down to his mouth. It was surrounded by his mustache and beard. Though they were both well kept, she wasn't sure she was a fan of so much facial hair. Still, she wouldn't pass up the chance to kiss him, beard or no beard.

At that moment, Deacon stepped back. He released her. When she glanced at him, he turned away. Did he know what she was thinking? Did he know that she'd almost kissed him again?

"I just need the olive oil," he said, as though nothing had happened between them.

"I think I saw some in the cabinet to the right of the stove."

"Thanks."

And that was it. They were both going to act as though sparks of attraction hadn't just arched between them like some out-of-control science experiment. Well, if he could pretend nothing happened, so could she. After all, it was for the best.

Refusing to let her mind meander down that

dangerous road, she focused on preparing a delicious dinner. In no time, Gaby filled their plates with seared steak, roasted potatoes and a fresh salad tossed with a wine-and-cheese dressing. They took a seat at the kitchen bar and ate in silence. In fact, Deacon was so quiet, she couldn't tell if he was enjoying the meal.

"Do you like it?" she asked.

"Yes." His gaze met hers but then he glanced away as though he wanted to say more but wasn't sure if he should. He stabbed a potato with his fork. "It's the best meal I've had in a long time."

"I doubt it. Mrs. Kupps is a marvel in the kitchen. But thank you for the compliment." It'd been a long time since anyone had taken notice of her cooking, including her father.

She was truly happy he was enjoying the meal. This is the point where she should once again probe him about the accident, but she just couldn't bring herself to ruin the moment. The questions had waited this long, surely they could wait a little longer.

They continued to eat in a comfortable silence. Deacon emptied his plate first. He politely waited for her to finish before he carried both of their plates to the sink. Together they cleaned up the mess they'd made in the kitchen.

After the dishes were placed in the dishwasher, Deacon said, "I should look over those notes for the fundraiser."

Gabrielle spied a beautiful sunset splashing the sky with brilliant pinks and purples. "Or you could go for a walk with me."

He shook his head. "I don't think so."

"Oh, please? It's such a beautiful evening."

He shook his head.

"Do you ever get out of this estate?"

He frowned at her. "Of course I do. I was just in the city today."

"I don't mean for business or whatever drew you away. I mean get out of here and do something relaxing."

"Not since the accident."

"Because of the paparazzi?"

He nodded. "It stirs up interest in me. And it's not my reputation so much as the people closest to me being harassed. When the reporters start their feeding frenzy, Mrs. Kupps can't even go to the grocery store without being harassed in the parking lot. I thought staying out of public sight would help and it did for a while."

"And then my father stirred things up."

Deacon lowered his gaze and nodded.

"I'm sorry." So he wasn't hiding out here for purely selfish reasons. "Is that why you gave your grounds crew time off?"

"Yes. It just got to be too hard on everyone. Although Mrs. Kupps refused to take paid leave. She said she wasn't going to let the reporters bully her."

Gaby glanced away. Guilt settled over her like a wet, soggy blanket. Here he was telling her how hard the media had made the life of those around him and she was writing daily reports for *QTR*. She was starting to wonder if her idea to publicly out him was the best approach.

"What's the matter?"

Her gaze lifted and she found him studying her. Apparently the guilt was written all over her face. "It's nothing."

"You're upset because I don't want to go for a walk."

It was best to let him think that was the source of her distress. "Oh, come on. There's no one out on the beach. Let's go."

"I thought the fundraiser stuff needed to be dealt with."

"It does. But there's plenty of time for it. Right now, I'd like to see more of this area. I must admit I'm not used to hanging out in Malibu. And the beach here is so nice. Come on." She reached out and grabbed his hand. "Show me around." She started toward the door, hoping that he'd give in to her tug of his arm.

"But there isn't much to show. It's a beach."

"A beautiful beach with a gorgeous sunset."

He followed her to the door and then stopped. "But I have work to do."

"Don't you ever just want to play hooky?"

There was a twinkle in his eyes. "So that's what you do? Play hooky instead of working."

The smile slipped from her face. She couldn't decide if he was being serious or if he was just giving her a hard time. She removed her hand from his. "I promise you that I work all day. I do a lot—more than what you've asked—"

"Slow down. I was just teasing you." He sent her a small smile.

She studied him for a moment, determining if he were serious or not. "Don't do that."

"Do what? Harass you a little?"

"Yes. Because I don't know you well enough to know if you're being serious or not."

"Perhaps I am too serious these days."

"You think so?" The words slipped across her lips before she could stop them.

His eyes widened. "I didn't know I was that bad."

"Let's just say that a bear with a thorn in its paw is more congenial than you."

"Ouch." He clasped his chest. "You really know how to wound a guy."

"Well, if you want to make it up to me, let's go for that walk."

He hesitated. She waited for him to say no, but instead, he said, "Fine. Lead the way."

She didn't say a word, not wanting to give him a chance to change his mind. Instead, she headed down the steps as quickly as her legs would carry her.

CHAPTER TEN

WHY EXACTLY HAD he agreed to this walk?

Deacon pulled the navy blue ball cap from his back pocket and settled it on his head. And even though evening was descending upon them, he put on the sunglasses that had been dangling from the neck of his shirt. These days, he always took precautions.

He shouldn't be out here, in the open for anyone to approach him—especially the press. The thought of being hounded with question after question about one of the most horrific events in his life almost had him turning around. Instead he pulled the brim down a little farther on his forehead. But the lure of stepping outside of his self-imposed confines was almost too tempting for him.

How could he resist walking along the sandy shore with the most beautiful woman he'd ever known by his side? The truth was, she'd cast a spell over him and he'd follow her most anywhere. And so he kept moving—kept in step with Gabrielle—as they made their way down to the beach.

He scanned the beach, looking for any signs of trouble. There was a man jogging along the water's edge. And coming from the other direction was an older woman walking her dog. Other than that, the beach was quiet.

Before his life had crashed in on him, he would jog on the beach each morning. And sometimes in the evening, if he had time. He'd come out here to clear his head. It was funny to think that he'd ever taken those simple liberties for granted—

"Don't you think?" Gabrielle's voice cut through his thoughts.

He had no idea what she'd been saying. "What was that?"

"I said the sunset is exceptional tonight. I wish I'd have grabbed my phone from the kitchen counter so I could take a picture of it."

Deacon stopped. This was one small thing that he could do for her. "I've got mine."

He pulled out his phone and snapped a picture. And then he handed it over so Gabrielle could forward it to her phone. When she was done, she returned the phone and that's when their fingers touched. How could such a small gesture get to him? And yet, a zing of nervous energy rushed up his arm and settled in his chest, making his heart beat faster.

"Thank you." When she smiled at him, it was like having the sun's ray on his face.

"You...you're welcome." It'd been a long time since he'd used his manners, but it made him feel more human—she made him feel like a man again. He didn't want this evening to end. "What are you waiting for? Surely you don't want to turn around already."

Her eyes lit up with surprise. "Certainly not."

They set off again at a leisurely pace. Every now and then they passed someone else with the same intention of enjoying such a perfect evening. Deacon couldn't recall the last time he was able to let go of the guilt, the remnants of the nightmares and the worry of what tomorrow would bring long enough to enjoy the here and now.

"I can see why you live here," Gabrielle said. "If I had the opportunity, I'd get a little place along here and wild horses couldn't drag me away."

"Actually I've been considering moving. It's time for a change. Maybe I could move someplace where they don't recognize me."

"I don't think that place exists."

He shrugged. "Perhaps."

"You aren't returning to the movies?"

Was she just being polite? Or had she not really looked at him? He stopped walking and held out his hand in front of them. "With scars like these, no one would want to hire me."

"These are from the accident?"

"Yes."

She reached out and ran her fingertip ever so gently over his skin. "It's not so bad. Maybe some makeup could hide what's there from the camera if you're self-conscious about it."

But makeup could not hide the scars in his mind. They were there—they kept him up at night, walking the halls in the dark. "It's not going to happen."

"Why not try?"

"Because…" Because he didn't deserve to be in front of those cameras any longer. She of all people should understand that. "Why are you being so nice to me?"

She shrugged and then started to walk again. "How am I supposed to act around you?"

"Like you hate me."

"Should I hate you?"

He inwardly groaned. Why did she have to keep turning things around on him? "It's not for me to say how you should feel. It's just that if circumstances were reversed, I'd probably act more like your father."

"And what has that accomplished? He has

broken the law and has his daughter bailing him out."

Deacon really wanted to understand her. "So you think by taking the high road that you'll accomplish more?"

"Such as you telling me what happened the night my aunt died?"

"There it is." He stopped next to an outcropping of rocks. "I knew that's why you dragged me out here. You wanted to get me someplace where you could interrogate me."

"That's not true. I didn't drag you out here—"

"But you can't deny that you didn't think about questioning me. You were hoping to wear me down into a confession."

Her gaze searched his. "Do you have something you need to confess?"

He should turn and leave. That's what he'd do if he were thinking clearly. That's what his attorney would advise him to do.

But his feet wouldn't cooperate. He stood there staring into Gabrielle's eyes and could only imagine the pain that she'd been through. And the not knowing, well, he knew all about that. Much too well.

He swallowed hard. "If I told you, you wouldn't believe me."

"Try me."

He wanted to trust her. He wanted to believe

that whatever he said would stay between the two of them. But he hardly knew her. And right now, he could count on one hand how many people he trusted.

Instead he turned and climbed up on the rocks. He made his way to a large boulder on the water's edge. He sat down, letting the sea breeze fan his face, and hoped the lulling sound of the ocean would ease the storm raging inside him.

He sat there for the longest time, trying to get his thoughts in order. By then the sun had sunk below the horizon. It was an overcast night with the moon peeking out here and there. Deacon found comfort in the long, dark shadows. He glanced around and found that Gabrielle hadn't left. Instead, she was sitting just a few feet away. She was too far away in the dark to make out her face. As she sat there with her knees drawn up to her chest, he couldn't help but wonder what she was thinking. He hated the thought that he continued to cause her pain. But nothing he could say would fix things.

"If you're waiting for a confession, you're wasting your time." He turned back to the ocean.

Gabrielle moved to settle on the rock next to him. "Is that because you didn't cause the accident?"

Why was he holding back? So what if she didn't believe him. Once he said it, it would be out there. Perhaps she'd believe him. Perhaps she wouldn't. But it was time he told the truth.

"I don't remember." Somehow it was easier having this conversation under the shelter of darkness.

"What don't you remember?"

"The accident." He could feel her intense stare.

"What part don't you remember?"

"All of it. They called it retrograde amnesia or some such thing."

"That's pretty convenient." She said it as a fact.

He turned to her and now that she was closer, he could make out the disbelief written on her face. "Actually, it isn't. I want to remember the accident as bad as you need me to remember. I need to know what I've done." His voice cracked. "I—I need to know if I'm responsible."

For a moment, Gabrielle didn't say anything. "So you're not holding out and trying to bury the events?"

His jaw tightened. He knew that she wouldn't believe him. But then again, why should she?

"No. I'm not lying." He shook his head. "I knew you wouldn't believe me."

"And the delay with the police report?"

"I've had my attorney pressing for its release, but without camera footage or an eyewitness account, it complicates matters. Once the police have finalized the report, it must go up the chain of command, ending with the DA's office. When my attorney checked yesterday, he was told the report should be released soon." When Gabrielle didn't say anything, he glanced over at her. "I'm sorry. I know that's not what you want to hear."

Her gaze met his and she placed a slight smile on her lips. "It's the truth and that's what matters."

"You believe me?" If she did, she'd be the first person to do so.

"Are you saying I shouldn't?"

"I'm just surprised is all."

Gaby paused. "So tell me more about yourself."

"You don't really want to hear about me?"

She nodded. "I do."

"Where do I start?"

"How about at the beginning."

"Well, I was born on Valentine's Day. My father died when I was thirteen. My mother finished raising me on my own. I split my time between the fishing boat and watching movies."

"Fishing and movies. Those are two diverse interests."

"The fishing wasn't a hobby. It was my job. I started when I was thirteen, getting paid under the table, in order to help my mother pay the bills." It hadn't been an easy life and his schooling had paid the price, but he'd graduated by the sheer willpower of his mother. "The movies were my passion. I drove my mother crazy telling her that one day I would be a movie star. And do you know what she told me?"

Gabrielle shook her head.

"She used to say, 'Deacon, you're a smart boy. You can be anything you want to be as long as you work hard and don't give up.'"

"She sounded like a smart lady."

"I thought so, too. And then she met my stepfather. In the beginning, he wasn't so bad. And then they got married. That was when I decided to move to California. I just couldn't stick around and watch those two argue. I tried to talk my mother in to coming with me, but she insisted that her place was with her husband."

"I'm sorry. That must have been tough on you."

"And what's even worse is that when she first found a lump in her breast, that—that man told her it was her imagination. By the time I talked her in to going to the doctor, the cancer was advanced. I brought her here to California. Oh, they tried to help her, but by then the cancer had spread."

Gabrielle reached out, taking his hand in hers. She gave a firm squeeze. It shouldn't, but it meant a lot to him. And it even meant more because she wasn't supposed to be here giving him support. She was supposed to hate him—hate his very existence. The fact that she didn't confused him, yet also intrigued him. There was definitely something different about Gabrielle.

CHAPTER ELEVEN

She didn't move.

Gabrielle left her hand securely within Deacon's hold. His hands were large and his fingers long. And his hand fit perfectly around hers. It was as though they were made for one another. Not that she was letting her heart get ahead of her mind. She knew that nothing could ever come of their relationship, whether he'd caused the accident or not.

Because in her father's mind, Deacon would always be responsible for her aunt's death. And she highly doubted that anything would change her father's mind. He was a very stubborn man. She'd inherited his stubborn streak. Or at least that's what her aunt had told her.

However, Deacon was far from the spoiled movie star that her father and Newton had accused Deacon of being. There was a lot more to this man than anyone would guess. He was like an onion, with layer upon layer, and she had an overwhelming desire to keep peeling back the layers until she reached his heart.

"Maybe we should head back." Deacon released her hand and got to his feet.

"So soon?"

He laughed. "We've been out here a long time. It's getting late."

"But we have the whole beach to ourselves." And then she dropped her voice. "We can do whatever we want and there's no one around to see."

"Be careful. Or I just might take you up on the invitation."

A shiver of excitement raced through her. She knew she shouldn't be flirting with him, but she couldn't stop herself. There was something about Deacon that she couldn't resist.

"Maybe I *want* you to take me up on the invitation."

Deacon stood there in the shadows. She wished she could make out his eyes. He was so quiet. Was he considering taking advantage of her suggestion? Her heart thudded against her ribs.

"Gabrielle, don't make offers you aren't ready to fulfill. Let's head back before something happens that we'll both come to regret. I don't want to hurt you."

He held out his hand to her and helped her

to her feet. For a moment, they stood there face-to-face. Her pulse raced and her heart pounded. With darkness all around them, a few moonbeams silhouetted Deacon's face. She wanted to tell him that she wasn't fragile. But her tongue refused to cooperate.

Instead of turning and heading back to the estate, Deacon continued staring at her. Was he considering kissing her again? Was it wrong that she wanted him to pull her against his chest and lower his head to hers?

And then he turned away and started climbing down off the rocks. When he was standing on the sand, he turned back to her and held out his hands in order to catch her. Even though she could make it down on her own, she didn't resist his offer of assistance.

He placed his hands on her waist and lowered her ever so slowly. Her body slid down over his. It was tantalizing and oh, so arousing. She was so caught up in the crazy sensation zinging through her body that she never noticed when her feet touched the ground.

Beard or no beard. Scars or no scars. Long hair or short. There was something magnetic about this man. She knew that it wasn't rational. And right now, she didn't care.

Her heart pounded so loud that it drowned out rational thought. She was going to live in the moment and damn the consequences. She tilted up her chin and lifted up on her tiptoes. Her mouth pressed to his.

His lips were warm and smooth. And the kiss, it was full of emotion, of need, of desire. Her hands slid up over his broad shoulders and slipped around his neck. She could get used to this.

Except for the beard. It tickled her. And when he moved to trail kisses down her neck, it tickled so much that she pulled away. A smile lifted her lips as she struggled not to laugh. He sent her a concerned look as though wondering if he had done something wrong.

"It's not you." But when he went to press his lips to her neck again, she placed her hands on his shoulders and held him back.

"What?"

She wasn't sure if he would take offense or not. And so she stood there not saying a word.

He frowned. "Just tell me."

"It...it's your beard. It tickles."

His eyes twinkled with mischief. "It does?" He leaned toward her. "How much?"

Before he could tickle her again, she yanked away from him. "Catch me if you can."

And with that taunt, she ran up the beach. A big smile was plastered across her face. For once, she wasn't the dutiful daughter working two jobs to keep the bills paid and she wasn't answering her father's numerous phone calls to check up on her. She was just Gabrielle Dupré, a woman with a dangerously handsome man chasing her. She could hear Deacon calling out to her, but she didn't stop until she was out of breath.

When she turned around, she fully expected Deacon to be standing there, but he wasn't. She squinted into the shadows. He was quite a way down the beach. What in the world? Hadn't he wanted to catch her?

Disappointment socked her in the gut. They'd been having so much fun. Where had it gone wrong?

Her wounded pride urged her to keep going. But another part of her wanted to wait and find out what was up. The curiosity in her won out. She started to walk back to him.

When she was within a few feet of Deacon, he said. "Sorry. I couldn't keep up. My leg is getting better, but it's not that good yet."

And suddenly she felt foolish. She was worried about him being upset with her when in fact he had an injury. It never even dawned on her that the injuries he'd sustained to his face, arms and hands had extended further.

"I'm sorry. I didn't think."

"It's not your problem. And how would you know?"

They started to walk side by side. She felt awful. She'd just assumed that he was fine. "Are you okay to walk back?"

"Yes. I'm just not up for running. Maybe one day, if I keep going to therapy and doing the exercises."

"You go to physical therapy?" She hadn't noticed him leaving on a regular basis, but then again, she hadn't been here that long.

"Not anymore."

"Why not?" She knew from her father's accident how important physical therapy could be to making a full recovery. "It's really important."

"I'm fine." His dismissive manner bothered her.

"If you were fine, you would have kept up with me or surpassed me. You are not fine. Your therapy is important. You can't just dismiss it because you don't want to do the work."

He arched an eyebrow. "And since when does my welfare matter to you?"

"It—it doesn't." Did it? She glanced away from him, not wanting him to read anything in her eyes. "But that doesn't mean it shouldn't be important to you."

"I don't think it's going to matter. All I do is haunt that place." He gestured toward the mansion in the distance.

"If you refuse to leave home, I can help you with the exercises."

"I don't need help." His voice rumbled with agitation, letting her know that she'd pushed as far as he was going to let her go.

And so they walked in silence. She wasn't sure what to say now. He'd made it clear he didn't want her help and he refused to go anywhere to get help. She couldn't believe this, but she'd met someone who was as stubborn or perhaps more stubborn than her father. They at least had that in common.

The thought of who could be more stubborn made her smile and the more she thought about it, a giggle started to form. And before she knew it, she was laughing. Maybe it was her nervousness or maybe it was the stress, but it felt good to laugh. Talk about a cathartic moment.

Beneath one of the estate security lights, Deacon stepped in front of her. "What's so funny?"

The frown on his face just made her laugh some more. It was almost like an out-of-body experience. She couldn't help herself. And it just felt so darn good.

"Stop it. Right now." His eyebrows were drawn into a firm line.

"I—I can't." She laughed some more.

She could see that the more she laughed the angrier he was getting. She really had to pull herself together. She had no idea what had come over her, but she needed to get a grip.

With a frustrated groan, Deacon turned and started to walk away. That was definitely not a good sign, at all. The elation in her started to ebb.

"Wait." She rushed to catch up with him, all the while trying to catch her breath.

"I don't care to be laughed at."

"I wasn't laughing at you. Not really." And then she thought about it a little more. "Well, maybe some. But it really wasn't that bad."

"I don't want to be laughed at."

Totally sober now, she said, "I just started thinking about you and my father and what you two have in common."

Deacon came to a stop and she almost ran in to him. "You were comparing me to your father?"

"Yes, in a way."

"What way?"

"You are both so stubborn. I was trying to figure out which one of you is the worst, but I couldn't decide."

"And that made you laugh."

"Yes, I guess it did."

He shook his head. "I don't understand you."

"That's okay. I don't really understand myself, either." It was the truth. She understood the parts of her that were like her father, but the other parts, the silly parts, sometimes surprised her. "I honestly don't know why I laughed. But once I did, it felt good. It's been a very long time since I laughed like that. You should try it some time."

He looked at her like she'd just grown an extra head. "You want me to laugh for no reason at all."

She shrugged. "Don't put it down until you've tried it."

He shook his head again. "It must be a woman thing."

Before they went their separate ways, Deacon asked for the fundraising plans. She ran upstairs and retrieved the papers. She was kind of hoping he'd follow her upstairs. His kisses were more addictive than the squares of chocolate with caramel centers that she enjoyed each night while reading.

She hurried back down the steps. "This is everything I have so far."

When she handed over the papers, their fingers touched. To her surprise, he didn't rush to pull away. Neither did she. Their gazes met and her heart careened into her throat.

Her gaze lowered to his mouth. She'd never been so tempted by anything in her life. What was it about this man that muddled her thoughts? It was as though he had some sort of magnetic force and anytime she was near him, she was drawn in.

And then he stepped back. "Thanks for these. I'll look them over tonight."

She choked down her disappointment. "Good. The sooner I jump on these plans, the better."

"Then how about a breakfast meeting?" When she didn't immediately respond, he asked, "You do eat breakfast, don't you?"

At last, she found her voice. "Yes, I do."

"Good. We'll discuss this in the morning." He gestured toward the papers. "Good night."

She stood there for a moment watching him retreat to the main house. What was wrong with her? She knew better than to fall for him. It was the ocean breeze and his deep voice that caused her to lose focus for just a few moments. She was fine now. Realizing that she shouldn't be standing around staring at Deacon like some besotted schoolgirl, she turned and headed up the steps.

Before it got much later, she needed to file

her daily report with *QTR*. She carried her personal laptop to a chair on her private balcony and sat in one of the comfy chairs.

She opened the laptop and typed in her password. Once she had her email open, the words came pouring out of her.

Tonight we walked on the beach. It was like a scene right out of a movie, with the lull of the water in the background and the gentle breeze. It was amazing.

Beneath the moonlight, we kissed. I don't think my feet were touching the ground. His touch—it was amazing. I know that I shouldn't feel anything for him because of the accident, but the harder I fight it, the more attracted to him I become.

His kiss awakened a part of me that I'd forgotten about. There was a rush of emotions unlike anything I've ever experienced before. It's all so confusing. Maybe I'm just lonely. It has been over a year since I dated anyone. Work and caring for my father has consumed my life. When I leave here perhaps I need to revisit the dating scene and update my online profile. Because there's no way what I'm starting to feel for Deacon is real. It can't be!

She read back over what she'd written. What was she thinking? She could never tell anyone her most intimate thoughts—most especially a tell-all magazine. Talk about creating sensational headlines.

With a shake of her head, she highlighted it all. Then she pressed the delete key. But she still had to find something to write in her report.

And after what she'd learned today, she was beginning to suspect there was no story here. But she had promised that she would document the details relating to the accident. And she liked to keep her word. So she started to write out in as much detail as she could what little Deacon had told her about the night of the accident.

But with every word she typed, guilt weighed on her. How could she betray Deacon's trust? Even if now it was to help *clear* his name?

Her emotions warred within her. She knew how Deacon felt about the paparazzi and tabloids. He would consider what she was doing as an utter betrayal. Could she blame him?

She hadn't taken any of this into consideration when she'd agreed to this plan. Getting close to Deacon, gaining his trust, was changing everything. And now she was utterly confused. More than anything, she wanted to leave. Each day that passed, her confusion over where she stood with Deacon grew.

Gaby saved her report to the drafts folder. She wanted more time to consider her actions. In the meantime, she jotted a brief email stating that there was nothing new to report.

She closed her laptop and leaned back in her chair. Her presence on the estate had nothing to do with the accident and everything to do with protecting her father from prosecution. And so she would keep her word to Deacon and stay until the fundraiser. And once it was a huge success, she could return to her life. A life without a brooding movie star with the ability to make her laugh and feel lighter than she had in years. Suddenly, returning to her prior life didn't sound so appealing. But life here on this Malibu estate wasn't reality. It was some sort of dream and soon she'd wake up— probably about the time the police report was released. And she worried about the steep fall back to earth.

CHAPTER TWELVE

MAYBE THIS HAD been a mistake.

Deacon sat across the table from Gabrielle. The table was done up with a light blue linen tablecloth. Fine china was laid out. The yellow napkins were folded into the shape of bow ties. A vase of yellow roses had been placed in the center. This was Mrs. Kupps's doing. The last time the table had been so fancy had been before the accident. These days, he ate at his desk with a tray of food. No flowers. No company.

What had he been thinking to invite Gabrielle to breakfast? Perhaps it was the fact that when she smiled, the whole world was that much brighter. And when they talked, she didn't hold back. She was filled with optimism. He gave himself a mental jerk. That line of thought could get him into trouble—big trouble. It was best to focus on the business at hand.

But that would be easier said than done with the table all decked out to impress Gabrielle. When he'd mentioned all the needless fuss to Mrs. Kupps, she'd clucked her tongue at him. She told him he needed to do everything he could not to run off Gabrielle, as she was the sunshine in his otherwise gloomy world. It was as if she was worried that he'd grow old alone. He was not some beggar, desperate for anyone's attention.

Is that what Gabrielle thought of him, too? Did she think that he was pathetic and deserving of her sympathy? He would show her. He did not need anyone's pity. He was not some charity case.

"You know this isn't going to work." His words came out terser than he'd intended.

Gabrielle glanced up from where she unfolded the yellow napkin and placed it on her lap. "Which part doesn't work?"

"All of it. Every single last piece of it." That wasn't exactly true, but he was in no mood to be generous. If they were adversaries, then perhaps she wouldn't feel obligated to be nice to him—to let him kiss her.

He watched her closely. He was waiting for her to leave. However, the only visible sign of her discomfort was in her eyes. They widened, but she didn't move. He knew a lot of people would have turned tail and fled by now. But not Gabrielle. She was made of sterner stuff. But he should have figured that when she'd volunteered to take her father's punishment.

She adjusted her napkin and at the same time avoided his gaze. When she glanced back up at him, she said, "I'm assuming you are referring to the fundraiser plans and not the meal."

"Of course."

She nodded. Then she set about removing the lid from the dish of scrambled eggs. She was going to eat? He was setting up for an argument and she was acting as though everything was perfectly fine. Everything wasn't fine.

He couldn't take her lack of reaction any longer. "Are you just going to sit there and ignore me?"

"I'm not ignoring you, but Mrs. Kupps went to a lot of work to prepare this meal and I think it'd be a shame to let it go to waste."

"You're hungry?"

She smiled at him. "Of course I am. I'm sure you'll feel better after you eat."

He wanted to disagree, but his gaze moved to her plate. The food did look good. "But what about the problems with the fundraiser?"

"They aren't going anywhere. We can deal with those later." She scooped up some bacon and added it to her plate. When he didn't move, she said, "Do you want some bacon?" When he didn't respond fast enough, she added, "If you don't hurry, there might not be any left. I love bacon."

He did, too. He held out his hand for her to pass the serving plate. She hesitated as though she weren't so sure she wanted to share, but in the end, she passed it to him.

It was really hard staying upset with her. She was either a very good actress, good enough to be in the movies with him, or she tried not to let things ruffle her. Either way, he was going to have to figure out a different way to deal with her. Because all his huffing and puffing didn't appear to deter her.

Gabrielle continued to fill her plate. "I can't believe Mrs. Kupps made us all of this food."

"She was more than happy to do it. For so long now, she's been begging me for things to do and I've been putting her off."

"I take it you don't have breakfast like this very often."

"No. Not at all. Not since, well, you know." He didn't want to bring up the accident. Not this morning. But since Gabrielle had entered his life, his appetite was back.

Gabrielle buttered her toast. "Well, I will make sure to tell Mrs. Kupps just how good this is."

"I'm sure she would love to hear it. I must admit that I've been lacking on the compliments lately."

"I'm sure she understands that you've been going through a lot."

When they'd finished their meal, which took much longer than he was accustomed to taking to eat, he found himself in a better frame of mind. He assured himself that it had nothing to do with what Gabrielle had said about him needing to eat, and more to do with the fact that he was right about this fundraiser and he would prove it to her.

Mrs. Kupps brought more coffee and then cleared the empty dishes. Both of them complimented Mrs. Kupps on the delicious food. The woman's cheeks grew rosy as she thanked them.

After Mrs. Kupps departed, Gabrielle turned to him. "Now, what were you saying about the fundraiser?"

"I don't think people are going to attend."

"Why would you think that? Are my plans that bad?"

He shook his head. "It isn't anything you've

done." Surely he didn't have to spell this out for her. "I'm the problem."

"Oh." Her good mood seemed to have diminished a bit. She sat there and stared off at the shimmering ocean for a moment. When she turned to him again, she had a glint in her eye. "Actually, I think all of your notoriety will work to our advantage."

He had a feeling he wouldn't like where she was going with this line of thought. But it was too late, he'd already been drawn down the rabbit hole. "How's that?"

"You forget that in addition to the car accident, you also have a movie being released next month."

"What about it?"

"I couldn't sleep last night, so I turned on the television. And guess what I saw?"

He sighed. "I don't know, but I'm sure you're going to tell me."

"I saw the promo for your movie. Your name and face were all over the ad. Your movie sponsors aren't backing down from using your brand and you shouldn't, either."

If only people still thought he was that man. Now they all questioned him and his actions—including himself. "I'm not that man anymore."

"Which makes people all the more curious about you—"

"I'm not going to be some sort of freak show for them to come here and stare at."

"Relax." She reached across the table and placed her hand on his. "I promise you, it won't be like that. I believe that people will come out for the event. They will want to get behind a great cause because so many lives have been touched in one way or another by breast cancer."

When she put it that way, he felt guilty for making such a big deal about his circumstances. Some people had it much worse. "So you'll make sure to keep the emphasis of the event on the reason for it and not on the sponsor?"

"Um, yes." Worry clouded her eyes. "Does that mean you don't want to be mentioned at all?"

"That is what I'd hoped."

She worried her bottom lip but didn't respond.

"Go ahead and say it."

"It's just that without your name, I don't know how to make the event stand out."

He reminded himself that raising funds would help save other families from having to go through the pain, the uncertainty and, for some, the loss of a loved one, like he'd experienced. And when it came down to it, if using his name would help raise awareness of the event, didn't he owe that to his mother's memory?

"Okay. You can use my name, if you think it will help."

"I do." Gabrielle pulled out a legal pad from a colorful bag she had on the ground next to her chair. There were handwritten notes on the top sheet. It was a long list. It appeared they were going to be here a while. She sent him a sideways glance. "You aren't going to change your mind after we get this all started, are you?"

He knew once news of the fundraiser was out there that his world would get a lot smaller, with paparazzi hanging from trees and sneaking onto the property. It would be chaos and he'd want to back out. "No. I'll manage."

"Good." A smile eased the worry lines bracketing her beautiful face. "And I think they are really going to have a great time."

He filled his coffee cup, then added a dash of sugar. He'd forgotten how much he enjoyed sitting outside in the morning with the bright sunshine and the cool breeze. He could feel Gabrielle's gaze on him. She was anxious to hear his thoughts, but he didn't think that she'd like what he was about to say.

As he stirred the coffee, his gaze skimmed down over the printout that Gabrielle had given him the night before. She had certainly paid attention to details and made certain that there was plenty of entertainment.

He took a drink of the dark brew and then returned the cup to the saucer. "You do realize that you have so many events listed that it dilutes the entire event."

Gabrielle's eyebrows drew together. "But people need something to do."

"True. But not this many things. This is more like an amusement park than a fundraiser." Before she could argue with him, he intended to prove his point. "You have golfing, amusement rides, clowns, artists, dancing and games. That's a lot. A whole lot."

"But with each of those things, we can raise money."

"How much money are we talking? Really?"

She sighed and gazed down over the list of events. "What are you proposing?"

"That you narrow the list down to two or three things."

She frowned at him. Then she shook her head and looked away.

"What?"

Her gaze met his as she worried her bottom lip.

"Gabrielle, just spit it out." He wasn't good at guessing, especially where women were concerned.

"I was just wondering if it is the money. You know, if sponsoring the event is too much for you."

Oh, that was all. This was something he could deal with.

"It isn't the money." Though this fundraiser would cost a small fortune to pull together, he could handle it. He'd had a number of blockbuster movies and he'd carefully invested the money. When her gaze told him that she still wasn't reassured, he said, "I promise. I'm good financially."

His main concern was for Gabrielle. She had invested herself completely in making this fundraiser a huge success. She had her hopes so high that when it all fell apart, she would have a long way to tumble.

In the short time he'd gotten to know her, he'd learned that she had a big heart—big enough to even care about his welfare, which was more than he'd ever expected. He didn't want her to get hurt because of him and his now tarnished reputation.

"That's good to hear." There was a catch

in her voice as though there were something more she wanted to say, but she decided to refrain.

"You know it's not too late to pull out—"

"No. I really want to do this."

He knew what she meant. She was anxious to get away from him. And he couldn't blame her. She blamed him for what had happened to her aunt. And as much as he wanted to deny it, he couldn't. He didn't know. And his nightmares only confused him even more.

He thought about just calling off the deal. But he knew Gabrielle would take it personally. She had a lot of pride and would think he didn't believe in her ability to pull it all together. He didn't want to do anything else to hurt her. So he would do what he could to help Gabrielle—even at the expense of his privacy.

Deacon cleared his throat. "The events should either be big draws in order to up the ticket price or garner large donations once the guests are in attendance." And he had another observation. "Perhaps keep this an adults-only event. Without children around, people will relax and perhaps they'll be willing to spend more freely."

"That's the exact opposite of how I ran my fundraisers for the library. I did a lot of activities to draw in the kids and by extension their parents." She frowned. "I suppose you're going to want to remove all of the fun events."

He really did hate to disappoint her, but he'd been around these affairs many times in the past. And he knew a lot of the big fish she was hoping to hook would appreciate something more low-key.

"Trust me." He knew that was a poor choice of words where she was concerned, but they were already out there and he couldn't undo them. So he kept going with the point he wanted to make. "I do know what I'm talking about."

"But it'll be boring."

He had to admit some of the charity events he'd attended were boring, but he didn't want to tell her that. He knew Gabrielle would use any excuse to keep her current lengthy list of events.

"Ah… I see. I'm right." Her face lit up.

"What are you talking about?"

"The look you just made when I said that it would be boring. You couldn't deny it."

"I was thinking is all."

"Uh-huh. What if we compromise?"

Oh, no. He had a bad feeling about this. His experience of compromising with a female in his private life consisted of him giving up on what he wanted, so the woman wouldn't be mad at him any longer.

With great trepidation, he asked, "What sort of compromise?"

And so they started with the first activity on the list—dart toss. They discussed it and the type of atmosphere they'd like to present to the people. In the end, it was cut in an effort to make the fundraiser more sophisticated.

After they made it through a quarter of the list and had nixed all but one item, Gabrielle said, "Okay. So we should stick to just a handful of entertainments."

"Or even less. For the most part, the affluent people you'll be inviting will want to be seen." He explained a little more of his understanding of the elite of Hollywood.

Gabrielle nodded. "Okay. I can work with this."

"Now, what were you considering for the main focus of the event?"

She took a moment, as though considering everything he'd told her. "I think we should make it a golfing event. Lots of people golf, both men and women. And you do have an amazing golf course."

"How would you know? It's a mess."

"Mrs. Kupps showed me some pictures. The course needs some TLC, but I talked to your head groundskeeper. He said that with the help of the entire grounds crew, they could pull it together. They might have to bring in some turf, but it is possible to have it together in time."

He arched an eyebrow at her. "You really have worked hard on this."

"I saw an opportunity and I took it. This fundraiser will be great—if you'll agree to it."

His gut told him not to do it. But he saw the gleam of hope in Gabrielle's eyes. He just didn't have it in him to turn her down. What would it hurt to get this place cleaned up? He wasn't even sure if he wanted to live here any longer. It would have to be restored if he were to put it up for sale. So he would let Gabrielle move ahead with her plans and when no one bought the tickets, he would still abide by their agreement. Once the planning was over, he would let her go back to her life.

He told her to take what they'd discussed and refine her list. Include a few more details and they'd go over it tomorrow. And then he would give her his decision about whether they should move forward with it or not.

He had a gut feeling that he'd dug himself a hole. Gabrielle had a determined look in her eye that said she would never give up on the fundraiser. And he was going to have to find a way to be okay with all those people being here on his estate.

Unless…no one bought a ticket or showed up. But then Gabrielle would be crushed and he would be to blame. Either way he would be in trouble.

CHAPTER THIRTEEN

THE PLANS WERE coming together.

Later that afternoon, Gaby straightened her desk. It had been a very productive day. She recalled her breakfast with Deacon. He hadn't been very congenial at first, but once he realized she wasn't going to give up, he became helpful.

And though she hated to admit it, he was right. This event needed a different vibe than the events she'd planned at the library. This was his world and he knew these people, so she'd follow his lead.

It may not be the type of event she was used to planning, but she would work to make it perfect. People would come. They would enjoy themselves, and they would donate to a worthy cause.

By five o'clock she'd also finished reading the screenplay Deacon had given her. She'd made a list of pros and cons and sent it to him in an email. With her tasks done for the day, she shut down the computer and then made her way to the guesthouse.

She brought the fundraising plans with her. She was too excited to stop now. The plans were coming together really well and instead of this event being her get-out-of-jail-free card, it was turning into an event she believed in and wanted to see succeed.

Mrs. Kupps had placed some dinner in the fridge with a note for reheating it. Gaby smiled. The woman was the absolute sweetest. She wondered if Deacon knew how lucky he was to have someone so kind and thoughtful in his life.

Gaby settled at the table with her laptop, a legal pad and all the notes she'd taken during her talk with Deacon. She didn't know how much time had passed when there was a knock at the door.

She couldn't imagine who it might be. Mrs. Kupps had left long ago. And no one could get access to the private estate.

Gaby ran a hand over her hair and a finger around her mouth, making sure there weren't any crumbs from the chocolate chip cookies that Mrs. Kupps had left her. And she rushed to the door. Gaby peered through the peephole and was shocked to find Deacon.

What was he doing here?

Her heart started beating faster. She glanced down at her white shorts and old Support Your Library tank top. Not exactly the most attractive outfit, but it'd have to do.

She swung the door open. "Hi."

Deacon looked uncomfortable as he shifted his weight from one foot to the other. "Never mind. I shouldn't have bothered you."

"It's fine. Do you want to come in?"

He shook his head. "I saw your light on and figured you couldn't sleep, either."

Either? As in he didn't sleep at night? Interesting. "I was going over more plans for the fundraiser."

"At this hour?"

"You gave me until tomorrow to come up with a revised plan."

"I did, didn't I?" When she nodded, he frowned. "If you need more time, it's not a problem."

"Actually, I'm just about finished. Tomorrow works fine to go over the agenda." She was certain that wasn't why he stopped over. "What did you need?"

He glanced down. There was a book in his hand. When his gaze rose and met hers, there was uncertainty in his eyes. "It was nothing."

"Obviously it was something or you wouldn't

be here. Are you sure you don't want to come inside?"

He shook his head. "I—I just finished reading this new book and thought you might enjoy it."

The fact he'd thought of her and wanted to share something personal filled her chest with a warm sensation. A smile lifted her lips.

She held out her hand. "What type of book is it?"

He handed it over. "It's a suspense book. But I'm sure you have other books you're already reading."

"Actually, I just finished one last night. So you have perfect timing."

"I do?"

She couldn't help but smile at his awkwardness. When it came to business, he was very sure of himself. But here, with it just being the two of them, he was nervous. And that bit of knowledge chipped away at the wall she'd erected to keep him out of her heart.

He shifted his weight from one foot to the other. "Usually I can figure out what's going to happen in the end, but this book kept me guessing until the last page."

She turned over the book and quickly read the blurb. "It sounds intriguing. I can't wait to read it. Thank you."

"I, uh, should be going." And with that he walked away.

As Gaby closed the door, she was struck by the gesture. It was so small and yet, it said so much about the man. The fact that he liked to read checked off a big box for Gaby—not that she was looking at him as a prospective boyfriend. But the fact that he used his mind for more than just work meant a lot.

And what meant even more was that he was thoughtful. The more she got to know him, the less he seemed like the monster that others had made him out to be after the accident. It was getting harder and harder to view him as the enemy.

"Okay. You have yourself a fundraiser," Deacon said the next day after going over her revised plans for the event in his office.

"I do?" Gabrielle smiled.

He tried to ignore the way her smile warmed his insides. *Focus on the fundraiser.* He cleared his throat. "Do you have a name for it?"

"Actually, I've given this a lot of thought. And you can change it, but how about the Diana Pink-Rose Tournament?"

The title that Gabrielle had chosen couldn't have been more perfect. His mother's name. She would have loved it. He was touched that

Gabrielle had included her name in it. A lump of emotion swelled in his throat and for a moment he didn't trust himself to speak.

Misinterpreting his silence, Gabrielle said, "If you don't like it, I could work on some other titles."

He shook his head and swallowed hard. He wasn't the type to let himself get emotional, but Gabrielle was the first person to do something so kind and thoughtful in honor of his mother. She probably didn't even know how much it meant to him and perhaps it was better that way. It's too bad the fundraiser would never become a reality. He thought it would definitely have been a great event.

His gaze met hers. "It's perfect. Thank you. What made you choose the pink rose for the title?"

She shrugged. "I guess because pink is the color of breast-cancer campaigns."

"Do you know what else pink rose means?"

She shook her head.

"Then come with me." He led her down to the rose garden, where he'd purposely planted a rosebush in every color that he could track down. As they made their way down the steps in the back of the house, he said, "My mother loved roses. And so I made a point of buying as many colors as I could find. I loved watching her face light up with every color that was added to the garden."

"That was very sweet of you. She was lucky to have you."

"No. I was the lucky one." And he meant every word of it. His mother had loved him even when he hadn't made the wisest choices. And she cheered him on when he reached for the stars. "I couldn't have asked for a better mother."

When they stood in the rose garden, Gabrielle's eyes searched his. "What are we doing here?"

"Did you know that each rose has a meaning?"

"I know that red roses mean love. But that's all."

"Ah, but not any love—true love. I'm sure you must get them all of the time."

"I must admit that I've never received any."

The fact that no man had given her roses really surprised him. Gabrielle was so beautiful. Her beauty started on the inside and radiated outward. He'd like to be the first to present her with one. "You should have roses and daily."

Color filled her cheeks. How was it possible that she grew more beautiful each time he saw her? His heart picked up its pace. He couldn't help but stare. He never got enough of looking at her. Was it possible for her to look even more radiant?

It was with great effort that he turned away. He walked down the brick path and stopped next to a white rose. "This one is the traditional rose of weddings. And it represents purity and virtue."

"How do you know all of this?"

"Each time I ordered a new rose, I would do my research. Roses are quite intertwined in history. I would distract my mother from her discomforts with stories that included the various roses."

Gabrielle gazed at him but didn't say anything. Yet there was a look on her face and he couldn't read it.

"What?"

"It's just that you continually surprise me."

"You mean you thought I was nothing but a conceited partygoer."

"Um, no. I don't know why you think that. It's just that I don't know any men who know so much about flowers."

His body tensed. It was even worse than he'd thought. "You think I'm a wimp—"

"No. Not at all. I think what you do here is wonderful." There was sincerity in her voice. She continued down the walk and stopped in front of a pink rosebush. "And how about these? What do they mean?"

"The dark pink petals mean gratitude and appreciation." He moved to a neighboring light pink rose. "And this one means sympathy."

He continued walking through the garden. When he came across his gardening supplies, he grabbed a pair of shears. He moved to some long-stemmed yellow roses. He searched for a perfect bloom and then cut it. He turned and presented it to Gabrielle.

A bright smile lit up her face. "Thank you." She lifted it to her nose and inhaled. "What does it mean?"

"Friendship."

She sniffed the petals again. "Is that what we have here?"

He hadn't tried to define what was going on between them until now. It was more complicated than friendship, but that title was safe and easy, so he went with it. "That's what I'd like to think."

Her eyes reflected her approval. "Me, too."

She'd slept in!

The next morning, Gabrielle awoke with a start. It was Deacon's fault that she'd been awake until the wee hours of the morning. He'd loaned her that book and it was good—no, it was great. She raced through her bedroom, trying to get ready for work as fast as she could. It wasn't that Deacon would be standing there by the office door waiting for her to arrive. It was more a matter of how much she wanted to accomplish that day.

She opened the door of the guesthouse and found a bud vase with a single yellow rose. She glanced around for Deacon, but he was nowhere to be seen. What had happened to the man who used to growl at her? She knew where she stood with his former self, but with this new version of Deacon, she was constantly losing her footing.

Deacon wasn't all good or all bad—he was both, but she was quickly learning that there was a lot more good in him than bad. She picked up the rose and lifted it to her nose. Its perfume was gentle but delightful. She'd never smell another rose without thinking of him.

She loved that each color of rose had a meaning. What impressed her more was that Deacon had learned the meanings in order to delight his mother.

As she carried the flower into the guesthouse to find just the perfect spot for it, her aunt's words came back to her: *if you find a man that is good to his mother, he will also be good to you.* Gaby had only been a know-it-all teenager when her aunt had given her these sage pieces of advice, but somehow they'd stuck. Someday, some woman was going to be very lucky to have Deacon by her side.

But it wasn't going to be her.

Even if she were drawn to him, the cards were stacked against them. There was just too much baggage between them. Relationships were hard enough under normal circumstances, but theirs was outside the bounds of normal.

As she tried to dismiss the profound meaning of Deacon making this gesture, she recalled what he'd said about yellow roses: *they meant friendship.*

Did that mean he considered her a true friend? The acknowledgment stirred a rush of emotions. She tried to tamp down her reaction, but her heart refused to slow. She once again breathed in the flower's gentle perfume.

The fact that it wasn't her birthday and it wasn't a holiday made this gesture all that much more special. He'd done it just because he could. This was the most thoughtful thing a man had ever done for her.

She knew then and there that she was in trouble. Deacon was working his way through all the barriers she'd built around her heart. Why did it have to be him that got to her? He was the absolute last person she should be interested in and yet, he was the one that kept her awake at night. And when she did fall asleep, he was the one that filled her dreams.

She was still puzzling over what to do about her feelings for Deacon when he materialized in the doorway of the office. He looked quite handsome. The dark circles under his eyes were fading and when he smiled, it eased the worry lines bracketing his eyes.

"I hope you had a good night," he said.

Gaby yawned. She didn't know if there was enough coffee in the world to keep her awake today. "Morning."

His eyebrows gathered. "Don't tell me you were working all night."

"No. I was reading." She recalled the book, so she grabbed it from her purse and handed it to him. "Thank you. It was just as good as you said it would be. It had me guessing right up until the last chapter."

He accepted the book. "I'm glad. But you didn't have to read it so quickly."

"Yes, I did. Once I started reading, I had to keep going. It's the way I am when I get into a book."

When he nodded in understanding, their gazes met and held longer than necessary, and her heart began racing. Her stomach shivered with nerves. She'd never had a problem speaking with anyone until now. When she glanced away from him, her gaze skimmed over the yellow rose. "Thank you for the rose. It's beautiful."

"I'm glad you like it." He stepped back and leaned against the desk opposite hers. "I've been thinking that you have everything pretty much planned out for the event except for the menu."

"I guess I need to do that sooner rather than later so I can give the caterer the menu." She pulled out a pad of paper. "Do you have a preference for the format? Sit-down? Buffet? Finger foods?"

He paused as though giving each option due consideration. "This is going to be more of a garden party than anything else, correct?"

Gaby wouldn't exactly classify the event that way, but for the lack of a better term, she went with it. "Sure." Following his line of thought, she said, "So the finger foods might be best." When Deacon nodded, she added, "And we could have the wait staff mingle with trays."

"Sure, sounds good."

There was one more thing that she'd thought of. She didn't know how Deacon would feel about it since he was in favor of streamlining the event. But she thought that it would add a bit of fun to the event and it could be a big revenue raiser during the afternoon.

"I've been going over the plans and I think there's one more thing we should do."

Deacon's face grew serious. "What would that be?"

"A Chinese auction."

"No."

She frowned at him. "How can you just readily dismiss the idea?"

"Because the basis of the Chinese auction is to ask others to donate items or services. I don't want to ask anyone for anything."

She dropped the pen to the desk and lifted her chin. "Maybe that's your problem."

"What's that supposed to mean?"

"It means that you're trying to get through this difficult part of your life by yourself—by putting a wall up between you and everyone else."

He arched a dark eyebrow. "I let you in."

"No, you didn't. I made my own way past your walls in spite of you."

"This is my life, my choices—not yours."

She glared at him. "And this is my fundraiser and I'm telling you that there will be a Chinese auction."

His voice lowered and rumbled with agitation. "Are you always so stubborn?"

"My father says so, but I don't believe everything he says." She no longer believed what he said about Deacon.

"And you're going ahead with this auction no matter what I say?"

"Yes."

"Then I won't waste any more time trying to talk you out of it." He muttered under his breath as he strode out the door.

Something told Gaby that he regretted giving her that flower. But she wasn't backing down. That was Deacon's problem. When he growled, everyone backed away. He needed to learn that life was about give and take.

CHAPTER FOURTEEN

THERE WAS SOMETHING different about Gabrielle.

Something not quite right.

Deacon had kept his distance from her since their disagreement last week. He didn't know exactly why he'd taken such a strong opposition to her idea of the Chinese auction. It wasn't a terrible idea. He could think of much worse.

He was left with no choice but to admit the truth to himself. He'd created the disagreement on purpose to put some distance between them. And it was all because of that rose and the other ones he continued to leave at her door each morning.

He had mixed emotions about leaving her yellow roses. Part of him said that it was just a friendly gesture, but another part of him wanted them to mean more. And that made him uncomfortable.

Logic said that there was a fifty-fifty chance he was responsible for the car accident. If he were responsible, Gabrielle wouldn't want anything to do with him. But even if he were found innocent, would that really do much to change their circumstances? He was still the other party in a two-party accident.

But when he was outside in the rose garden, he would catch glimpses of Gabrielle. And when she didn't think he was watching, the smile vanished from her face. A glint of worry reflected in her eyes. Was it his fault? Had he upset her that much?

This time he didn't need to hear her aunt's voice in his head to know he needed to somehow fix things. Mrs. Kupps was right about Gabrielle being a ray of sunshine in his otherwise gloomy life. And when her light was dimmed, the darkness and shadows were too much for him.

He approached Gabrielle where she was sitting on the patio. She had pen and paper in hand, but she wasn't looking at either. Instead she was staring out over the ocean with a faraway look in her eyes.

"Mind if I join you?" He stopped next to the table.

She blinked and turned to him. "I don't mind, if you don't."

It wasn't exactly the invitation he'd been hoping for, but he sat down anyway. "Something is bothering you. I'd like you to tell me what it is."

She shook her head. "I'm fine."

"No. You're not. You haven't been happy in a while."

She sighed. "I didn't know that it was that obvious."

"Maybe not to others, but I've gotten to know you pretty well and I know when you have something on your mind. Is it the fundraiser? Are you worried—"

"No. It's not that. Things are going well. In fact, I'm already getting RSVPs to the digital invitations."

Frankly, that was quite a surprise to him. He'd assumed the event would be a failure. Actually, he'd been counting on it. The thought of opening his home to all those people was not something he relished, but it was a problem he'd deal with later. Right now, he was concerned about Gabrielle.

"If it's not the fundraiser, what it is? Maybe I can help."

Her tentative gaze met his. "It's my father."

"Your father? I don't understand. Did something happen?"

"No. At least not that I know of."

He should probably leave it there. It wasn't like he was friends with her father. But the sadness on her face had him searching for the truth. "Then what is it?"

"We've just never been apart for this long. It's always been just the two of us against the world."

Deacon hadn't expected this. "But isn't it nice not to be responsible for caring for him on a daily basis?"

She shrugged. "It never really bothered me. Maybe it should have. I guess I like being needed."

She did? "You mean you don't mind taking care of your father even to the extent of you not having a life of your own?"

"Is that what you think?"

"Well, when was the last time you had a date?"

She glanced away. "It's been a while."

"And when was the last time you did anything with your friends?"

"Lindsay and I went to the movies the other month."

"Other month? That sure doesn't sound like a busy social calendar."

"Why do I need a busy social calendar? So what if I don't have time to hang out. I have two jobs to hold down. And the cleaning and shopping to do." She paused as though she realized that she'd said too much. And then she frowned at him as though he was now the one in trouble.

He drove home his point with one final comment. "Maybe you take on too much."

"I do what I need to do."

There was no talking to her. She obviously couldn't see that she did so much for others that there wasn't any time left for her. He felt bad for her, but his persistence on this subject was only upsetting her more. "I didn't mean to upset you."

She sighed. "It's not you. I'm just frustrated. I'm not sure my father is taking proper care of himself."

This was Deacon's chance to pay her back for all the generous things she'd done for him. And he knew exactly what he must do.

When he looked at Gabrielle, he knew he didn't have any other choice. "Go to your father."

Her head jerked around until her puzzled gaze met his. "But our agreement—"

"I know about our agreement and I don't care. I won't stop you. Go to your father. Make sure he's okay."

"Really?" Immediately her face lit up. "You don't mind?"

"No." He was lying.

He knew that once she passed beyond the estate gates that she would not return. Why should she? She had a life that had nothing to do with him. She had a father that loved her. Friends to do things with. She had a full life.

And what did he have to offer her? He struggled to come up with any reason for her to return. The memory of their kisses passed through his mind. But he knew that had been a fleeting thing—a moment of pity on her part for a man who looked and sounded like some sort of beast.

"Do you mind if I go now?" She looked radiant, like Dorothy about to click her red heels.

He, however, didn't feel like the Wizard. "No. Go."

She ran over to him and hugged him. The moment passed much too quickly and then she pulled back.

He refused to let her see how much her departure bothered him.

Without another word, Gabrielle rushed away. He wasn't even sure that her feet touched the ground, she was so happy to get away from there. How could he take that happiness away from her? He sighed in resignation.

He was happy for her, but he was sad for himself. He just couldn't believe in the short amount of time that they'd been together that she'd come to mean so much to him.

And now he was on his own again.

CHAPTER FIFTEEN

It HAD BEEN a lovely visit.

The weekend had flown by. It had been so good to see her father. The time with him had been exactly what she'd needed. And best of all, Newton had been out of the house. Everything had gone smoothly so long as she stayed away from the subject of Deacon.

She'd tried a couple of times to let her father know that Deacon was treating her really well, but her father hadn't wanted to hear any of it. All he'd wanted to hear regarding Deacon was if she'd gained any information to help move along the legal process. He was still convinced that Deacon had paid off people to bury the accident report. In the end, Gaby had given up because she didn't want to spend the short amount of time she had with her father arguing. Though she didn't believe Deacon was a monster, she couldn't confidently claim his innocence, either. They still didn't know exactly what had happened in the accident. To say she was confused was putting it mildly.

While she was home, she'd cooked for her father. She'd spent quite a bit of time in the kitchen preparing healthy meals. By the time she left, the fridge was full. The freezer was stuffed with meals that just needed reheating. And her father's prescriptions were refilled.

Her father begged her not to return to Deacon's estate, saying that he could take whatever punishment the judge was likely to throw at him. But Gaby told him this was about more than just him. She was doing important work with the fundraiser and she needed to see it through until the end. And that soon she would be back home. With a hug and a kiss, she'd left for the long drive back to Malibu, knowing her father was doing quite well on his own. Perhaps she did fuss over him more than necessary.

Thanks to Deacon, both she and her father were finding that they didn't need each other quite so much. When her time was over at the estate perhaps she could stick her foot back in the dating pool. But as soon as she thought of dating, Deacon's image came to mind.

She tried to imagine him with his hair cut

and his face shaved. He'd look like a whole new man and perhaps he'd feel like one, too. Maybe it was time to see how he felt about a makeover.

Monday morning, she opened the door to the guesthouse of Deacon's estate and paused to look around. After waking up for the past week to find a yellow rose at her door, today there was none. It saddened her, but she knew eventually they had to stop. Still, she'd come to look forward to them. And now she tried not to read in too much to their absence.

It wasn't until later that morning, with a check in hand for his signature, that she went in search of him. At that hour of the morning, Deacon was usually tending to the roses. But when she went to the garden, there was no sign of him and it didn't look as though he'd been there that morning. That was odd.

She went to his office, thinking he was working on an important project, but the office was empty and the lights were off. Concern started pumping through her veins.

In the kitchen, she tracked down Mrs. Kupps. "Do you know where Deacon is?" The woman nodded, but her face said that something was definitely amiss. "You're worrying me. Where is he?"

"He's closed in his rooms."

"His rooms. But why?"

"I don't know. He hasn't said a word to me." Mrs. Kupps shrugged. "He went in there after you left and he hasn't come out. I'm worried about him."

Gaby recalled their last conversation. She thought things had been fine between them, but then she recalled how Deacon had been eager for her to go visit her father. She'd missed her father so much at the time that she hadn't paid much attention to Deacon's reaction, but looking back on things, she should have realized something was off with him.

"Leave it to me. I'm used to dealing with stubborn males."

A weak smile lifted the worry lines on the woman's face. "I knew as soon as I laid eyes on you that you would be the ray of sunshine this house needed. I was just preparing him a late breakfast. You could take it to him, if you like."

"Thank you. I would."

Mrs. Kupps put together a tray of eggs, bacon, toast, fruit and juice. When she handed it over, she said, "Good luck."

"Thank you. I'll need it."

Remembering the day that Deacon had taken her to his room to clean her wounds from falling in the rose garden, Gaby made her way upstairs. The tall double doors were closed, but that wasn't going to stop her.

She leveled her shoulders and then gave a quick knock. Without waiting, she opened the door. She was surprised to find the room so dark. She squinted into the shadows, looking for him.

"Go away!" His deep voice rumbled through the room.

It seemed that he'd regressed. "Your growl isn't going to scare me."

Suddenly he was standing in front of her. Frown lines were deeply etched upon his face. "You're back?" He seemed surprised.

"Of course."

His face quickly returned to its frown. "Well, since you aren't going to leave until you've had your say, get it over with. Quickly."

"I hear that you've been in your room since I left. What's the matter? Are you sick?"

"No."

"Something must be the matter." Now that her eyes had adjusted to the low lighting, she moved to a table and placed the tray. "You have things to do. There's no time for slacking."

"I'm not slacking." Again his voice rumbled. "Now go away. Shouldn't you be with your father?"

So *that's* what was bothering him? She

worked to subdue a smile. He had missed her. Who'd have guessed that? In truth, she'd missed him, too. But she wasn't ready to admit it.

She moved past him with sure, steady steps. At the window, she stopped and threw open the heavy drapes, letting the bright morning sun into the room. She turned to find Deacon squinting and trying to block the sun's rays with his hand.

"Close that."

"And let you sit in here in the dark? I don't think so."

He grunted his displeasure. "I'm your boss. You're supposed to do what I say."

"I'm your friend, remember? And I'm doing what's best for you."

"No, you came back because your father probably kicked you out for working here. I bet you don't listen to him any better than you do me."

"When both of you make poor choices, I don't mind calling either of you out on them."

Deacon frowned at her. "I didn't make a poor choice."

"You mean sitting around in the dark is your way of being productive?"

He opened his mouth and just as quickly closed it again. He sighed and glanced away.

"If you're going to stay here, shouldn't you be in your office doing some work instead of harassing me?"

"I will just as soon as you start eating that delicious meal Mrs. Kupps prepared for you." He looked at her but he didn't move. She crossed her arms and tapped her foot. "I have all day."

With a look of resignation, he moved to the small table and sat down. "You are certainly something."

"I'll take that as a compliment."

He took a bite of egg. It was followed by a half a slice of toast. Partway through his meal, he stopped and looked at her. "Why do you care?"

"Because you apparently need someone to care about you. You don't seem to do a very good job of it on your own."

"How am I supposed to, when I know what I've done?" The worry and stress lines etched his handsome face.

"I thought you said you didn't remember the accident?"

He let out a heavy breath, causing her heart to lodge in her throat. Did he know more than he'd told her? Had the police report been released? Her mind rapidly searched for the reason for his despair.

"Talk to me," she prompted, needing him to tell her that the worst hadn't happened.

"The nightmares are getting worse. It's hard to tell the truth from the products of my imagination."

"And…" She waved her hands as though trying to pull the information from him.

"And I remember bits and pieces, like the fire burning my skin. I remember your aunt. I remember her saying 'Take care of Gabrielle.'"

"What? She did?" When he nodded, she asked, "Is that why you gave me this job?"

His gaze met hers. "Yes."

Gaby had been right about him. Deacon was a good man—buried beneath a mountain of unnecessary guilt. Her aunt's words were the proof of his innocence that she needed.

"Why are you smiling?" His dark eyes searched hers.

"Don't you understand? You're innocent."

His eyebrows drew together and his forehead wrinkled. "Why would you say that?"

"Because if you were guilty, my aunt never would have asked you to reach out to me and take care of me—not that I need you to." Gaby smiled at him, feeling as though a huge weight had been lifted. When he didn't look convinced, she asked, "What's wrong?"

Deacon rubbed the back of his neck. "Your theory is not proof—not legally."

"It's enough for me. It'll all work out. You'll see." There was one more thing bothering her. "But if you really wanted to fulfill her wishes, instead of having me work here, you could have just offered me money or something, but you didn't. Why?"

Deacon hesitated. "When you went on and on about how you cared for your father after telling me that he could take care of himself, I wanted you to know that you could have a life of your own and you didn't have to sacrifice everything for him."

"It was more than that and you know it."

"Perhaps."

"Perhaps nothing. You wanted to separate me from my father in order to punish him for the pain he caused you."

Deacon's gaze lowered and he nodded. "Yes, I did. I suppose that makes me a bad person."

"No. It just makes you human." She eyed him as he returned to eating. "Speaking of making you more human. What would you say to a haircut and shave?"

"I don't think that's a good idea."

She wasn't going to let him wiggle out of this. He'd been hiding behind all of that hair long enough. "Really? You like having your hair hang in your eyes?"

"No, but it's better than seeing what's beneath it."

So he was worried about the scars. He couldn't hide from them forever. Maybe facing up to them would be his first step back to the life he'd left behind after the accident.

She stepped closer to him. "I'd like to see you. The real you beneath all of that hair."

He looked at her as though gauging her interest. "And what if I'm a scary mess?"

"I'll still think you're handsome." Now where had that come from? She couldn't believe she'd uttered those words, even if it was the truth.

His eyes widened with surprise. "Really? You're not just saying that because you pity me? Which is ridiculous considering I lived and your aunt didn't. Listen to me. I just keep rambling…"

She kneeled down next to him. With her hands, she smoothed his hair back from his face. "There you are. Yes, you're definitely the most handsome man I know."

There she went again, saying the first thing that popped into her mind. But this time, when Deacon reached up and wrapped his hand around her wrist, she didn't regret speaking the truth.

"Okay. I'll do it," he said, "as long as *you* do the haircut and shave."

That wasn't exactly what she'd imagined when she'd proposed the idea. Still, if he was willing to take this big step with her, who was she to deny him?

CHAPTER SIXTEEN

HER HEART POUNDED in her chest.

After gathering the supplies she needed, Gabrielle stood there in Deacon's bathroom holding a razor.

What if she messed up? She wasn't a barber or a hairdresser. Sure she could trim her own bangs when her hairstyle dictated. But there was a big difference between trimming bangs and trimming a man's entire head, on top of giving him a shave.

But with his dominant hand still not working well enough for him to manage a razor, what choice did she have?

Call a professional? The idea was so appealing and yet, she knew that it was an impossibility. Deacon was so certain that beneath all of that hair that he was a monster. And this was her one chance to prove him wrong.

The truth was she didn't know what she'd find beneath his beard. She prayed that in his mind, he'd made the scars much worse than they were in reality. No matter what he looked like, she had to let him know that he wasn't some sort of beast.

The fact that he trusted her enough to allow her to shave and trim him wasn't lost on her. They had come a very long way since she'd started working at the estate. She remembered how awkward it felt working in that office, knowing that he was on the other side of a locked door.

But at the time, she hadn't understood that he had such significant injuries from the accident. That certainly wasn't how the accident was portrayed in the news. In fact, she was beginning to think that nothing in the media was as it seemed.

"Did you change your mind about revealing the real me?"

Deacon's voice jarred her out of her thoughts. "No. Of course not. I'm just trying to decide if I should start with your hair or your beard."

"The hair. That way after you're done shaving me, I can jump in the shower."

"You're sure about this?" She had to hear his answer one more time.

"I am." He studied her for a moment. "If you are."

"I am." She sucked in a calming breath. It

didn't work, but she focused on the task at hand instead of her lack of experience.

Trading the razor for a pair of scissors, she set to work. She drew on her memories from her own haircuts and her experience trimming her dad's hair when he was in rehab. Gaby took her time, not wanting to mess up. She knew there was a lot riding on this particular haircut.

Her stomach was a nervous, jittery ball of nerves. Lucky for her, her hands remained steady. A cut here. A cut there. The trimmed locks of hair piled up on the floor. And all the while, Deacon remained quiet.

She walked around his chair, checking for any uneven spots. There was one by his left ear. With great care, she trimmed it.

And in the end, he retained both ears, and no blood was shed. It wasn't the most stylish haircut, but considering his hair before, it was a large improvement.

Deacon lifted a hand and ran it over the short strands.

"Do you want to look in the mirror?"

"I don't have any mirrors. I got rid of them."

"But I have one." She held up a hand mirror.

He turned away and shook his head. "I'll see it when you're all done."

After the trimmings were swept aside, she grabbed a comb and the scissors. Then she set to work trimming his beard as short as she could. She'd never trimmed a man's beard before. Sure, she'd shaved her father when he'd been in the hospital but his stubble was nothing compared to Deacon's full-on beard.

But what got to her more was being this close to him. There was something special about him. It was more than him being a famous movie star. It was an air of strength and power that exuded from him. And she was feeling herself being drawn closer and closer to him.

She'd never experienced such an intense attraction and it scared her. Not the part about her father or the accident. No—it was the fact that she didn't know how she was going to return to a world without Deacon's reluctant grin, or seeing the way his eyes twinkled when he was happy.

As the fundraiser grew closer, her time with Deacon was running out. She wanted this time to count. If all she had left when this was over were the memories, then she wanted them to be earth-shattering, pulse-quickening memories.

Deacon didn't know how much time had passed.

His eyes were closed as he focused on Gabrielle's gentle touch. He didn't know that a haircut and shave could be so tantalizing. Thank goodness she didn't attempt to make small talk because he wasn't sure he'd be able to follow along.

Each time her fingertips brushed over his skin, it short-circuited his thoughts. And each time her body brushed up against him, he longed to reach out and pull her onto his lap. He ached to press his mouth to hers. He smothered a groan.

"Are you okay?" Gabrielle paused.

He opened his eyes to find her staring directly at him. "Um, yes."

"You're sure?"

She'd heard him moan? He smothered a curse. He thought that he'd caught himself. Deciding it was best that he change the subject, he asked, "How's it going?"

"Before I go any further, I need to soften your beard." She turned on the water.

He couldn't see, but he could imagine Gabrielle letting the water get hot and steamy. And the next thing he knew, she was draping a hot towel over his jaw. The heat gave him a bit of a start, but he soon adjusted to it.

All the while, he was tempted to ask for her mirror just to make sure his hair wasn't an utter mess, but then he decided at this point, it didn't matter. If worse came to worse, he'd shave his entire head. At one point in his life, his hair had only been touched by the finest stylist in the movie business, but that felt like a lifetime ago. These days his hair didn't matter to anyone.

Gabrielle moved in front of him. "I have to admit I've only ever shaved my father when he was in the hospital."

"Don't worry. I trust you." It wasn't until the words crossed his lips that he realized what he'd uttered. He would retract the words if he could. But now they were out there. They filled the room with silence as the heavy impact settled in.

Gabrielle immediately turned away so he was unable to read the emotions filtering through her expressive eyes. When she turned back, she removed the hot towel from his jaw.

He didn't know why he'd said such a thing. That wasn't exactly the truth. He knew. He just didn't want to admit it to himself or to anyone else.

He was a man who prided himself on relying on no one. He told himself during all these months of solitude that he was fine on his own because he couldn't trust anyone else in his life. And then Gabrielle burst into his world and little by little she'd chipped away at the crusty shell that he'd armed himself with.

And now he was starting to care about her. He didn't know what to do with these feelings.

But it was getting difficult to ignore his body's strong reaction to her with her fussing all about him. And when she stood in front of him to shave him, he had to close his eyes to keep from staring at the most tantalizing view of her firm breasts. But it was too late. The image of her curves straining against the thin cotton top when she leaned toward him was permanently tattooed upon his mind.

Think of something else—anything else.

He didn't want to let Gabrielle know just how much this session of playing barbershop was getting to him. The truth was he was letting himself get too close to Gabrielle. And no matter how he tried to hold her at arm's length, she ended up getting so much closer. But that would all end as soon as Gabrielle revealed his scars.

He told himself that he was ready for her to be repulsed, but he wasn't. One look at him and she wouldn't be able to pack fast enough. The truth was that before Gabrielle, he'd forgotten how to smile—how to laugh. He'd forgotten what it was to sleep at night for more than two hours. She had totally turned his life upside down and made him think of all the things that he could still do.

"Relax." Gabrielle's voice drew him back to the present.

"I am relaxed."

"No, you're not. Your jaw is rigid and so are the muscles in your neck. If you don't trust me—"

"I do trust you. Keep going. I have things to do." The truth was he didn't have any other place that he wanted to be other than right here with her hands moving gently over his skin.

"Look at me when you say those words."

He opened his eyes and found her staring straight at him. "I trust you."

With that admission hanging between them, she continued shaving him. Her motions were slow and deliberate. He banished the worries and drew in a deep, calming breath. The more she worked on him, the more relaxed he became under her skilled hands. He sat there with his eyes closed, enjoying the way her fingers felt on his skin. Her touch was gentle, but it ignited a fire within him.

She ran a towel over his face. "You can open your eyes. I'm done."

When his eyes opened, she was smiling at him. "You're already done?"

"Already? That took close to an hour."

"It did?"

She nodded. "And it was worth every minute. Because just as I predicted, you're amazingly handsome. You'll have all of the women swooning at your feet," she added softly.

"I doubt it." He ran a hand over his smooth jaw. It felt so good to have all that hair removed. The beard had been itchy and too warm.

However, he refused to let himself buy in to Gabrielle's compliment. He'd seen the damage to his face at the hospital. He'd been a mess of angry scrapes and nasty gashes. She was just being nice.

"If you don't believe me, have a look for yourself." She handed him a hand mirror.

He really didn't want to look. He knew that he'd find an angry red map of scars. Still, it couldn't be avoided forever. He might have removed all the mirrors from his home, but he was quickly learning just how many surfaces were reflective.

Not allowing himself an easy out, he lifted the mirror. He blinked. Surely he wasn't seeing clearly. He turned his head to one side and then to the other. Where were all the ugly scars?

"See, I told you." Gabrielle continued to smile at him. "You're as handsome as ever."

"I can't believe it." He ran his fingers over his face. "I know that when they transferred me to another hospital, they mentioned something about bringing in a world-class plastic surgeon, but I didn't think there was any hope of salvaging my face."

"I'd say that surgeon is quite gifted."

The angry red lines had faded. The surgeon had hidden most of the scars. Others were fine white lines, but they didn't make him look like Frankenstein. He'd never be the way he used to be, but at least now he wouldn't scare children.

He turned to Gabrielle to thank her for helping him through this difficult step. But when he faced her, the words caught in the back of his throat. She looked at him differently. Not in a bad way. More like a woman who desired a man. Was that possible? Or was he reading what he wanted in her eyes?

As though in answer to his unspoken question, she bent over and pressed her lips to his. At first, he didn't move. He didn't want to do anything to ruin this moment. And yet she pulled back, ever so slightly.

Need and desire pumped through his veins in equal portions. When she looked at him, he felt like a whole man. Not like a man haunted by his past and worried about his bleak future. She looked at him as if she couldn't imagine him doing anything bad. And he so wanted to believe it, too.

Giving in to the urgent need consuming his body, he slipped his arms around her waist and gently pulled her back to him. Her warm, soft curves pressed against his hard muscles and a moan formed in the back of his throat.

He didn't know why fate had brought them together, and in this moment, it didn't matter. The only thing he cared about was Gabrielle's happiness. He wanted to give her a good memory—something to overshadow some of the pain he'd caused.

In all honesty, the memory they were creating would be something he'd cherish, too. He'd never known anyone as generous of heart, as understanding and as bossy as Gabrielle. And he knew no matter how long he lived, he'd never find anyone else like her.

As their kiss deepened, he longed to have all of her. But he had to be sure she wanted the same thing. He wouldn't rush her.

With every bit of willpower, he pulled back and waited until her gaze met his. "Are you sure about this?"

She nodded.

That wasn't good enough, he had to be absolutely sure she wanted him as much as he wanted her before he carried her into his bedroom and laid her down on his king-size bed. "Gabrielle, do you want to make love?"

"I thought I made my desires clear just a moment ago."

"I need to be sure. I… I don't want to do anything to upset you."

Her eyes reflected the desire warming his veins. "Then let me make this perfectly clear. I, Gabrielle Dupré, want to make love to you, Deacon Santoro."

That was all he needed to hear. He scooped her up in his arms and carried her to the bedroom. He laid her gently on the bed. Nothing had ever looked so good—so right.

He knew after tonight that nothing would ever be the same for them, but he would deal with the aftermath later. Much, much later…

CHAPTER SEVENTEEN

THE NEXT MORNING Gaby awoke alone.

She reached out, running her hand over Deacon's pillow. It was cold to the touch. Her gaze searched the bedroom. There was no sign of him.

The convergence of disappointment, embarrassment and sadness left her grappling to keep a lid on her emotions. He regretted their night together. A sob caught in the back of her throat.

No. Don't lose it now. You're stronger than this.

As she looked to see the time, her gaze stumbled across a yellow rose on her bedside table. It hadn't been there last night. She was certain of it.

She withdrew the rose from the vase. As she stared at its velvet petals, she wondered what Deacon was trying to tell her. Did he want to go back to being friends? Or was she reading too much in to it? Maybe, in this case, a rose was just a rose.

She glanced at the clock. She realized if she didn't hurry, she'd be late to work. Finding out where her relationship now stood with Deacon would have to wait until later. She was expecting phone calls that morning about the fundraiser. And no matter what happened between her and Deacon, she intended to do her best job.

She scrambled out of bed and rushed to get dressed. There was something else she needed to do that morning—conclude her arrangement with *QTR*. She may not know the exact circumstances of the accident, but she knew Deacon hadn't been at fault and didn't deserve any further bad press.

When she returned to the guesthouse, she knew she'd made a big mistake. Not the night she'd spent with Deacon. One minute, he'd been so tender and loving. Then in the next moment, he'd been hot and passionate. It was a night of surprises and delights. No, her problem was agreeing to do an exposé about him. Now that she knew about her aunt's request, she was certain he was innocent. Her aunt would never have asked a killer to look after her. And now Gaby had to try to undo some of the damage.

So far *QTR* hadn't printed anything that she'd given them, not that there was anything noteworthy. Hopefully it wasn't too late to call off the arrangement.

Gaby retrieved the number of the editor at *QTR*. The phone rang and rang. She began to worry that no one would answer.

Suddenly there was a male voice. "Hello."

Gaby was startled. This certainly wasn't the perky young female editor that she'd been assigned to. "I'm sorry. I must have rung the wrong number."

"This is Elle McTavish's desk."

Gaby swallowed down her nervousness. "I was hoping to speak with her."

"And who is this?"

"Gaby, um, I mean Gabrielle Dupré. And who is this?"

"Thomas Rousseau."

As in Quentin Thomas Rousseau II. Gaby's stomach clenched. Oh, boy. She'd heard stories about the man. None of it was any good. He was legendary. She wasn't sure what was going on, but she had the feeling that it wasn't going to be good.

She gripped the phone tighter. "Could I leave a message for Ms. McTavish?"

"I've taken over for her."

But he was the owner, not an editor. Gaby clenched the phone tighter. "I see. Then perhaps you are the person I should speak to."

"I'm listening."

"I've changed my mind about doing the story about Deacon Santoro."

"I see." His voice was smooth and patient. "But my understanding was that's what you wanted—for the world to know about Santoro—and how he's evading the law."

At the beginning, that was exactly what she had wanted. But now she knew that her aunt hadn't blamed Deacon and, therefore, neither should she. He was not the beast she'd originally thought. He was just a man—a man who had punished himself needlessly.

"That was before—"

She stopped herself from saying too much. The less she told this man, the better. She had learned firsthand how words and images could be twisted into something they're not.

"Before what?"

"It was an accident. That's all."

"Have the police said this?"

"No, but they will."

"Miss Dupré, what changed your mind about gaining the truth and forcing the police's hand in delivering their findings about the incident?"

She worried her bottom lip. What was she supposed to say now? She didn't want to break

Deacon's confidence. She didn't want to share her aunt's last words with the world.

"Miss Dupré?"

"I want to end our arrangement."

"Is that because you're now romantically linked with Mr. Santoro?" The man's voice took on a hard edge. "Yes, I saw that photo of you in his arms. I was not happy to be scooped by another magazine."

"It wasn't the way it looked." At least at *that* moment, everything had been innocent. Now everything was exponentially more complicated.

"Tell me about it." His tone was more congenial. He wanted her to give him a story but she refused to do it.

"You and I don't have a signed agreement. Remember, your magazine wanted to wait until you could ascertain what information I would provide."

"There was a verbal agreement, was there not?"

"Sounds like a case of 'he said, she said.'"

Regretting the deal she'd struck with the magazine, and now this man that she didn't trust in the least, she said, "I am calling off the arrangement. Besides, I never gave you anything you could use."

The line went dead.

She had to admit that had gone a little better than she'd expected. And as she set aside her cell phone, she felt a bit lighter. She didn't care how hard up she was for money, she was never working for a gossip rag again.

Now she had to deal with Deacon. She had no idea what to make of his disappearance that morning. He did say that he didn't sleep much. Maybe he'd just gotten up early.

And to complicate matters, she needed to come clean about her liaison with *QTR*. She felt now that her relationship with Deacon had shifted, she needed to be completely open and honest—even if he didn't like what she was about to say.

How was he supposed to face her after last night?

Deacon moved to the window in his office. She was going to look at him differently. She was going to expect things of him—things he couldn't give her.

And yet he didn't want to lose her. He told himself that it was the fact she was the best assistant he'd ever had. And this fundraiser, if it worked out, might help fund a breakthrough in the fight against breast cancer. There was too much riding on them continuing to work together.

Was it possible to wind back the hands of time? If they didn't talk about it, could they pretend that amazing night of lovemaking had never happened?

"Deacon, we need to talk."

He didn't move as he stared out the window of his office. She'd just said the five words he'd been dreading. It was time he put his plan in action.

Deacon turned to her. "I wanted to talk to you, too. I have another screenplay and I'd like to get your thoughts on it."

"It can wait—"

"No, it can't. If I don't get the rights to it, someone else will. I know it."

"But what I have to say—"

"Can wait." He saw the frustration reflected in her eyes. He owed her more than a quick brush-off. He swallowed hard. "I wasn't expecting last night. It wasn't something I planned."

"Me neither."

That was good to hear. It meant she had to be as confused as him. "Then you'll understand when I say I need time to process this. My life—it's not the best time to start anything serious."

Disappointment dimmed her eyes. "I understand. But I feel I owe you the truth about something."

Revealing secrets and truths were things people did when they were establishing a relationship. When they were building a foundation. He didn't intend to do any of those things with Gabrielle. Because when that police report was released—when he was sure his whole world would come crashing down—he didn't want Gabrielle hurt any more than she already would be.

Whatever she'd done or thought she'd done, it wouldn't compare to his transgressions.

"Now isn't the time for sharing." He averted his gaze. "We can talk another time."

"But—"

"Please." She didn't know how hard she was making this for him.

Because in a different place, at a different time, under different circumstances, he would have welcomed her into his life with both arms. Turning her away was the hardest thing he'd ever done.

As he watched her walk away, he felt the distance grow between them. It was like the sun had been eclipsed from his life. And as much as he wanted to go after her—to pull her into his arms—his feet remained rooted to the floor.

He clung to the fact that she was better off without him.

CHAPTER EIGHTEEN

It was all coming together.

Beneath the blue skies, Gaby stood to the side of the golf course and gazed out over the estate grounds. Deacon's grounds crew were miracle workers. Of course, it helped that they'd enjoyed months of paid leave and were now anxious to get back to work. Gaby couldn't imagine what it would be like to have all that free time. Right now, she didn't have enough hours in the day to do everything that needed done.

And ever since they'd made love, Deacon had held her at arm's length. She didn't understand it. Had she done something wrong? Had he not enjoyed it? Whatever it was, he wasn't talking and she was left with nothing but doubts and worries. Thankfully the fundraiser was only a couple of days away and there were so many last-minute details to attend to that she didn't have time to get lost in her thoughts.

Every last ticket for the event had been sold. Now if only they'd all show up. The food had been ordered. The catering service had been reserved. The rose garden was already in order. Deacon had seen to that. But there was something she was forgetting. She just couldn't put her finger on it.

"You wanted to see me?" Deacon's voice came from behind her.

"I did." She tried to hide her surprise at him actually seeking her out instead of calling her on the phone. "What do you think?"

"About what?"

She subdued a sigh. What was wrong with him? "Look around. The grounds are done. The men have been working on it every day from dawn until dusk."

Deacon remained quiet as he took in his surroundings. His expression was masked behind a look of indifference. How could that be? Didn't he notice what a mess the estate had been? Even she had been out here every day going over the details to make this place spectacular.

"It looks good." He still didn't smile.

"Good? That's it. This place is amazing. Anyone would be amazed by the transformation." There was something more to this. Something that he wasn't telling her. "Deacon, we need to talk about the other night—"

"There's nothing to talk about."

She was tired of being patient—of thinking he just needed time to adjust to the change in their relationship. "I don't believe you."

"What?" He gave her an innocent look.

"Don't go acting like you don't know what I'm talking about. You've been avoiding me at all costs ever since we made love."

"I've been busy." His phone chimed. He withdrew it and held it up as proof of his business. Then he silenced it and slipped it back in his pocket.

"Fine. We'll play it your way."

"I'm not playing. What happened was a mistake. One we shouldn't repeat."

She managed a shrug as she wasn't so sure she trusted her voice. It took her a second to swallow the lump in the back of her throat. With a blink of her eyes, she mustered up what she hoped was a blank expression. He wasn't the only actor here.

Willing her voice not to waver, she said, "And the golf course? What do you think of that?"

"It's good."

She planted her hands on her hips. "After all this work, *good* is all you have to say?"

His gaze didn't meet hers. "I don't know what you want me to tell you."

"More than that. My lunch was good. Your haircut is good. But the transformation of this estate from an unruly jungle to a work of art is spectacular."

He sighed and then proceeded to rub the back of his neck. "I just can't shake the feeling that something is going to go terribly wrong." He turned to her and apparently her thoughts were reflected on her face because he said, "What happens if the report on the accident comes out between now and then?"

"We deal with it."

"What if it says I'm to blame?"

In all honesty, she wasn't sure how she'd cope if the report really did say that Deacon was responsible for the accident that stole away her aunt, no matter how sure she was that he was innocent. But now Gaby understood why he'd pulled away from her. The accident was like a deep chasm between them, and try as they might, it was hard to cross.

She wanted to believe she would be able to move past the accident—to not hate him if the truth turned out to be different than what she imagined. But she knew that emotions could be tricky. Her father was a prime example—who'd have thought he would be arrested for stalking and harassment? Her father had never been in trouble with the law before in his life.

Not wanting to get caught up in the what-ifs and maybes, she said, "Would you like to give it a go?" She gestured toward the golf clubs that were all spiffed up and standing next to the house in a special shed. "The clubs are just waiting to be used."

He hesitated and she was certain he was going to turn her down. And then he said, "I'll do it, if you do."

She shook her head. "Not me."

"Why not?"

"I—I prefer to watch." She really didn't want to admit that she didn't know a putter from an iron. Those were terms she'd heard the groundskeepers throwing around.

Deacon arched an eyebrow as he stepped closer to her. "Are you afraid I'll beat you?"

He was challenging her? Oh, boy. Maybe it was time for her to fess up. "No. I'm not worried." There was a glint of excitement in his dark eyes. He definitely had the wrong idea and so she said, "I don't know how to golf."

His eyes widened. "But you're the one who suggested making this a golfing event."

"I know I did. You did happen to notice that

most of your yard is taken up by a nine-hole golf course?"

"But usually when you host an event, you know how to do the said event."

Now she understood his confusion. "But see, I'm not the host, you are. The fundraiser is in your mother's name. This is your home. And the people are coming here because of you—"

"No. They are coming because they are curious to see the recluse and find out if I'm an ugly, scarred mess like the tabloids have portrayed."

"Whoa! Whoa!" She waved away all his worries. "That isn't why they're coming here. They're attending the event to support a worthy cause."

"And I think you see only the good in people."

"What's that supposed to mean?"

"Look at you. You're always so positive. Wanting to believe people are truly good. But they aren't."

She didn't know where all of this was coming from. "I'm not some Pollyanna."

"Yes, you are. You're all smiles and sunshine."

She hadn't meant to mislead him. "I'm human just like you. I have my share of doubts and worries. I just try not to dwell on them."

He rolled his eyes.

"Don't do that. Don't make me out to be like someone up on a pedestal."

"Then tell me that you aren't doing everything you can to convince yourself that I'm innocent. Go ahead. Deny it."

"But my aunt—"

"She was probably in shock. She probably hadn't even understood what had happened. The only thing she could think about was her love for you."

She shook her head, refusing to believe his version of events. "Now that I've gotten to know you, I just can't believe you would be reckless with your life and that of others."

"But see, that's the point. I have been in the past. I've bought super cars and I've taken them out on the road to see how fast they could go—to push the envelope. Doesn't that make me reckless?" When she couldn't argue with him, she remained quiet. His gaze implored her to affirm his actions. "Go ahead, say it."

"No." She wasn't going to help convict him when there wasn't any evidence. Because if he were guilty—if he did act recklessly—she would have lost not one but two people that she cared deeply about in that accident.

"Gabrielle, you can't bury your head in the

sand and pretend the accident didn't happen. The reality is my nightmares grow stronger every night. You have to accept that—that I'm responsible for what happened. No amount of positivity will be able to overcome the fact that I—I killed your aunt."

Each word he threw at her was a blow at her heart. Tears pricked the back of her eyes. "Why are you doing this?"

Deacon hated hurting her.

But he didn't have a choice. More of his memories were starting to come back to him. He remembered being in the car. He recalled the blinding headlights headed straight for him. The rest was bits and pieces, but he couldn't shake the guilt mounting within him.

And now he was making a mess of things with Gabrielle. He'd only wanted to help her. He should have done it from a distance. Bringing her here to his estate was his first mistake. The second mistake was getting caught up in her greenish-gray eyes and letting himself be drawn in by her pouty lips. Now he had to untangle the ties that bound them together. It was best for Gabrielle.

He cleared his throat. "I never should have let things get this far. You and I need to part now, before either of us gets hurt."

"Are you saying you never cared? That this thing between us is all in my imagination?"

Why did she have to make this harder on herself? He couldn't tell her what she wanted to hear—not if he wanted her to leave, if he wanted to save her from more pain.

"It was fun and nice." He glanced away, unable to stand the hurt reflected in her eyes. "But it wasn't real. It would never last."

His phone vibrated again. What in the world was going on? His email was busier than ever. Using his phone as an excuse not to face the pain he'd caused Gabrielle, he pretended to check it. In truth, he couldn't care less about business right now—right when he was sending away the woman that he'd come to care about deeply—

The breath caught in his throat as his gaze strayed across a bit of news. There was a distorted picture of him with ugly scars, next to a photo of Gabrielle. The headline read, The Beast Wins Beauty?

"What is it?" Gabrielle asked. When he didn't respond, she asked again, "What's the matter?"

He ignored her as his gaze skimmed down over the slanderous piece of trashy journalism. The fact that Gabrielle was *quoted* in the article stabbed him in the chest. Each breath was painful.

All this time, he'd thought she was so amazing with her ability to see the good in him. At first, he hadn't wanted to believe in her generous heart, but she'd worn him down and snuck past the wall around his own heart. And it'd been a lie. All of it.

"Deacon, I'm getting worried. What's wrong?"

His gaze narrowed in on her. "Why? Are you hoping I'll give you another headline?"

"What?" She reached for his phone. The color drained from her face as she read the article. When she looked up at him, worry lines bracketed her eyes. "I can explain."

"Don't bother." His angry words died in his throat when he realized she'd done what most anyone would have done in her situation. "I probably would have done the same thing in your place."

"But you don't understand. I—I backed out of the deal. Once I knew you better and you told me what my aunt said to you, I backed out."

He wanted to believe her but he couldn't allow himself. "It looks like you gave them plenty to work with."

"This isn't my stuff. They did a hatchet job

on the information I supplied them. Please. You have to believe me."

Anger pulsed through his veins. He was angry at the tabloid for printing outright lies. And he was furious with himself for not listening to his gut. Instead, he'd let down his guard with Gabrielle. He'd let himself fall for her and it'd all been a lie.

"Just go." His voice rumbled.

"But the fundraiser—"

"Is taken care of. You said so yourself. All the arrangements have been made. Now that your end of our deal has been fulfilled, it's time for you to leave."

When she didn't move but rather stood there with tears glistening in her eyes, he said with a low guttural growl that he knew she hated, "Go now. And don't come back."

He turned his back to her because it was killing him to send her away. He would try to forget the happiness that Gabrielle had brought to his life. He would banish the image of her warm smile—a smile that she would get when he walked in the room.

Because none of it had been true. While he'd been falling in love with her, she had been figuring out how best to twist the knife. And she'd succeeded. Worst of all, he deserved it and more after causing the accident.

His last little bit of hope that his name would be cleared was also gone. The future looked bleak. He just hoped the article brought Gabrielle and her father some sort of satisfaction.

CHAPTER NINETEEN

THIS WAS THE absolute last place he wanted to be.

Deacon stood off to the side of his newly manicured lawn. Despite what he'd said to Gabrielle, the estate did look spectacular. She hadn't overlooked a single detail. And his staff had gone above and beyond to make everything perfect for this occasion.

After Gabrielle left, it had been too late to cancel the fundraiser. He knew it was up to him to see it through to the end. Only things weren't turning out quite as he'd imagined.

With not one, not two, but three scandalous headline articles in as many days that featured him in the worst light, he didn't think anyone would attend. Instead, everyone was in attendance. He didn't know if they'd come in spite of the article or to find out if any of the lies were true.

The only person not there was the one person he longed to see—Gabrielle. He knew he should be angry with her, yet when she said that she'd backed out of the arrangement with the magazine, he'd believed her. But it didn't mean they belonged together.

He drew his thoughts up short. Today he had to be a gracious host.

He really couldn't believe all of these people had shown up. There were fellow actors, directors, pillars of the music industry and people he didn't recognize, but what they all had in common was that they were happy to be here. All were smiling, talking and greeting each other. Food and drink flowed freely. The golf course looked better than it ever had, thanks to Gabrielle's insistence.

He'd already had compliments and slaps on the back that his scars had healed so well. After that doctored photo in *QTR*, where they'd made him to look like some sort of monster, people were pleasantly surprised by his normal appearance. It felt surprisingly good to greet friends and acquaintances. And he had Gabrielle to thank.

A mariachi band played in the background as well-dressed people mingled. Deacon worked his way past the crowd. He was headed for the rose garden, hoping to gain a moment alone.

Though people had been accepting of him, it was all a bit overwhelming.

And then Gabrielle appeared in the distance.

Deacon came to a halt. It couldn't be her, could it? Not after the way they'd ended things. He blinked and looked again.

She was gone.

He expelled a disappointed sigh. It must have been someone that resembled Gabrielle. He assured himself it was for the best. She would soon forget him and move on with her life.

And then Gabrielle came back into view. She had on a yellow crocheted dress. The spaghetti straps showed off her slim shoulders. The plunging neckline hinted at her voluptuous breasts. He swallowed hard. A slit ended high up on her thighs, letting the crocheted high-low skirt show off glimpses of her long legs. She really was a looker.

It was then that he noticed a man next to her. The guy was chatting her up. Deacon stood too far away to overhear what was being said, but Gabrielle was smiling. However, it wasn't an easy smile. It looked forced. Yet, the guy acted as though he didn't have a clue she was only putting on a show of being nice to him.

Deacon's body stiffened as this man had the audacity to reach out and put his hand on

Gabrielle's upper arm as though they knew each other intimately. If Gabrielle's body gestures were anything to go by, the attention was unwanted. Deacon started forward. Before he reached the two, the guy leaned over and whispered something in Gabrielle's ear. She pulled away. What did the man think he was up to? Couldn't he tell Gabrielle wasn't interested?

Deacon's steps quickened. He would step in. Or should he? He slowed down. Was it his place to step in? After all, he had told Gabrielle to go away. What would he be telling her if he were to step in now?

Yet, this was his estate. He had a right to see that none of his guests were unduly harassed. Determined that he had a right to make sure things were all right, he continued in Gabrielle's direction. He could see that she was no longer smiling and her gaze was darting around as though to find an excuse to slip away from the guy.

Deacon was almost at her side, when someone stepped in his way, blocking his view of Gabrielle. "Excuse me."

"Deacon, old boy. It's so good to see you."

Deacon focused on the man speaking to him. It was his agent. A man he used to speak to at least once a day, but since the accident, his agent hadn't bothered to call. The man had obviously given up on Deacon, figuring his pretty face was gone forever. Now that his face had healed, Deacon wondered if his agent realized he'd given up too soon.

"Harry, it's good to see you." Deacon did his best to smile, even though he didn't feel like it—not for a man who, for all intents and purposes, had told him in the hospital that his future in Hollywood had gone up in flames along with his good looks. Of course, Harry had been smart enough to put it in friendlier terms, but that's what it amounted to.

"You know I've been trying to reach you—"

"I've been busy." Deacon knew whatever Harry wanted would be what was good for Harry and not something that would help Deacon. "Could you excuse me for just a moment—"

"Not so fast. We should talk. This fundraiser was a brilliant idea. It certainly squashes those rumors of you becoming some sort of recluse. I've never seen the estate look better. And you, well, it's remarkable. If I hadn't seen you in the hospital, I'd never believe the extent of your injuries."

"The plastic surgeon did an amazing job," Deacon murmured tightly.

"Indeed. And this event is a great chance to

get you back in the swing of things. Everyone seems to be having a great time."

"My assistant gets the credit. This fundraiser was her brainchild." It wasn't until the words were out that he realized Gabrielle was no longer his assistant. She was…well, they no longer had any sort of official relationship, but it sure didn't feel that way to him when he saw that other guy hanging all over her. Where had she disappeared to?

"This assistant, she sounds like a miracle worker," Harry said. "Perhaps I should try to steal her away from you."

The forced smile slipped from Deacon's face. "I don't think so."

"Well then, I'll get straight to the point of my calls. I have a part in a movie that I think you'd be perfect for—"

"No."

"No?" The agent's mouth gaped. "But surely you want to get back to work."

"I am working. I'm finding that I like being behind the camera more than I like being in front of it."

"So the rumor is true?"

"Yes. I'm starting to back some movies, and I'll see where things go from there."

The agent nodded as he digested the information. "If you change your mind, give me a call."

"I don't think that will happen." Deacon had to admit it felt good to know what he wanted in life. And what he wanted most was Gabrielle—even though he couldn't have her.

The agent's eyebrows rose with surprise before his face settled into a smile. "I knew you weren't one to hold a grudge. Glad to hear all of the ugliness is in the past." And then as though the man didn't know what else to say, he said, "Well, I should be moving on. I have other people that I need to speak to."

Deacon didn't say a word, not wanting to waylay the man. After the man moved on, Deacon's gaze scanned the area for Gabrielle. He didn't see her. But there were so many people that she could be anywhere.

He started moving through the crowd, but it was slow going with so many people wanting to greet him. He did the obligatory handshakes and pasted a smile on his face. But he didn't linger. He needed to find her. He needed to—to what? Make sure she was okay? And then what?

He wouldn't know the answer to that until he caught up with her. He stopped and turned in a circle looking for her. She had to be here. And he wouldn't stop until he found her.

CHAPTER TWENTY

SHE SHOULDN'T BE HERE.

But she couldn't stay away.

To Gaby's surprise, the morning after she'd left the Santoro estate, the complaint against her father had been formally withdrawn. He was free and clear. There was no reason for Gaby to ever see Deacon again—but seeing him was exactly what she had planned.

She owed Deacon an apology. Instead of helping him with this fundraiser, she'd only made things worse for him. *QTR* had issued a series of malicious articles about Deacon. She recalled the morning's headlines on the *QTR* magazine. It was all over the newsstands, grocery stores and internet: Beast Hides from Public & Justice.

It appeared that *QTR* was intent on running a series of damning articles about Deacon. It killed her to read how they'd stolen her words. *QTR* had twisted the facts and made up other things. They'd embarked on an all-out campaign against him. No wonder she hadn't spotted Deacon amongst his guests. The fact that he had even let the fundraiser go forward amazed her.

When he'd banished her from the estate, she'd worried that he would once again hide away in his darkened office and keep everyone outside the tall estate walls. And after those atrocious headlines, she wouldn't blame him if he cut himself off from the outside world.

She didn't care what Deacon said, she knew he had a good heart. She couldn't—she wouldn't—accept that he'd recklessly taken her aunt's life. It had been a horrible accident. End of a very sad story.

She'd been talking frankly with her father—something she should have done before things had gotten out of control. And the fact that her father had agreed to attend the fundraiser with her was the first step on the road to forgiveness, even if her father would vehemently deny it. He said he was only here because Gaby had planned the event. He refused to acknowledge that the event had anything to do with Deacon.

Her gaze scanned the enormous crowd of finely dressed people. Was Deacon really somewhere among them? She had to try and fix things. She at least had to try. She didn't like the way they'd left things.

"Hey—" Newton nudged her "—isn't that the guy that acts in *The Screaming Racers*?"

She hadn't seen the action movie, but she had seen the previews on the television in her father's living room. "Yes, I think it is."

"What do you think he's doing here?"

"Supporting a good cause."

"I don't know. He's a big star. Why would he come here to the beast's lair?"

"Newton, don't start."

"Hey, it's what they called him in the headlines. You know, the story you helped write."

She gave Newton a stern look. "I only agreed to bring you here because you insisted that my father might need help getting around. But we could leave now—"

"Okay. Okay."

He pressed his lips together into a firm line. But his eyes told a different story. If she wasn't careful with him, he would make a scene. She sincerely regretted bringing him. As soon as she placed some tickets in the raffle baskets, she'd gather her father and Newton and they would go.

"Go find my father. You know, the reason you're here?" she said. "I need to go buy some raffle tickets."

"I'm hungry. Maybe we'll get some food." Newton walked away.

With Deacon nowhere in sight, Gabrielle made her way over to the table where they were selling the tickets for the twenty-five elaborate baskets that had been generously donated by area businesses.

Gabrielle couldn't help but smile as she observed all of the people gushing over the beautiful baskets and buying an arm's length of tickets at a time. This event was turning out better than she'd ever imagined. She wished Deacon could find some comfort in knowing that these people were in attendance in spite of the nasty headlines. That had to mean something, right?

With guests still streaming through the gates and the press along the road photographing the event, this was certainly going to give Deacon some positive spin. She pulled her cell phone from her purse. She clicked through to the different social-media sites to find that Deacon's name was trending. And this time, his name was linked with positive news.

Her lips lifted into a broader smile.

She'd done it. She'd kept her word to Deacon. The fundraiser appeared to be a smashing success. But this event wasn't nearly enough to make up to him for the lies that were lining every grocery store checkout and splattered on the internet. If only she could explain properly, maybe he'd believe her.

But where was he? She'd already worked through the crowd of guests and walked the whole way around the estate. And now, she was back where she'd started, in the garden. There had been no sign of Deacon amongst the pink tea roses, the purple climbing roses and the many other varieties of blooms that took root in the impressive garden.

The truth was she shouldn't have left when he'd told her to. She should have…well, she wasn't sure what she should have done. But leaving hadn't been the right answer. Because every minute she was away from him, the gap between them yawned even wider. She hoped it wasn't too wide for her to cross. Because she missed him with every fiber of her body. Life wasn't the same without him in it.

And then she remembered something her aunt had told her way back when she was in elementary school. There had been some trouble between her and another girl. Her aunt's sage advice was that a gentle word or a kind action could be more powerful than the strongest objection or the harshest retaliation. Her aunt had been a gentle soul. And Gabrielle had a feeling that her aunt would understand why she was doing what she was doing with Deacon. Or at least she hoped so.

"Hey, Gaby! Wait!"

It wasn't Deacon.

Her heart sunk a little.

With a forced smile, she turned to find Newton running back over to her again. "I thought you went with my father to find the food."

"Your father found someone to talk to and I decided to bring you a drink."

She realized now that he must have had more than one himself. He lurched toward her, spilling the drink on her bare arm, and then making as if to pat her dry with his free hand, surprising her.

Gaby turned, jerking away from his touch. "Stop. I'm fine…"

It was then that she spotted Deacon. He noticed her at the same time. Newton was still talking, but she was no longer paying attention. Her full focus was on Deacon.

"Excuse me." She moved past Newton and headed straight for Deacon.

Please let him listen to me before he throws me out.

CHAPTER TWENTY-ONE

GABY'S STOMACH SHIVERED with nerves.

As Deacon approached her, she forgot about everyone else around them. In that moment, it was just the two of them. She started moving toward him. Although the closer she got to him, the more she noticed the tenseness of his body and the rigid set of his jaw. She braced herself for a confrontation. She understood how he'd think that she'd turned against him.

They stopped in front of each other. At the same time, they said, "I'm sorry."

Gaby's gaze searched his. "Do you mean it?"

He nodded. "I never should have told you to leave like that."

"And I should have stayed. I need to tell you how sorry I am—"

"You!" Newton wedged himself between her and Deacon. "You killed her aunt. You should be in jail."

A hush fell over the growing crowd.

"Newton! Stop." Gabrielle saw the pain that his words had inflicted on Deacon.

Newton turned on her. "How can you defend him?"

Gabrielle's gaze went from Newton to Deacon. If there were ever a time to be honest with herself and everyone else, it was now. "I'm defending Deacon because I've come to know him. I know that he's a good man with a big heart. He would never intentionally harm a person." She turned to Deacon. She stared deep into his eyes. "I know this because I love him."

"You can't. He's a killer." Newton shouted the accusation.

By then a crowd had formed around them. People were pulling out their cell phones and filming the scene. This mess had gone from bad to worse.

"He's my best friend," she countered.

"Don't," Deacon said. "I can defend myself."

"I'm only speaking the truth," Gaby said, feeling very protective of him.

Before Newton could say another word, Gaby's father rolled his wheelchair between them. He turned to Newton. "That's enough."

"But he is a—"

"Hero," her father said.

"What?" Newton stared at her father like he'd spoken another language.

Her father cleared his voice. "I should have said something earlier. The official accident report was released this afternoon. There is irrefutable proof that Deacon is innocent."

"What evidence?" Deacon approached her father.

"I'll admit my protest in front of your place may have been rash, but it garnered a lot of attention." He held up a hand, staving off Deacon's heated words. "Before you say anything, it was that protest and those interviews that brought forward a reluctant witness. They have a video of the accident. It has cleared you, Deacon. My sister was the one that swerved into your lane."

Gaby reached out and took Deacon's hand in hers. She smiled through her tears. At last this long, hard journey was over.

She turned to Deacon. "Did you know about this?"

He shook his head. "I haven't touched my mail or listened to my voice mails today. I was busy making sure all of your plans for the fundraiser were carried out."

Gaby's father turned to Deacon. "And I owe you a big apology. Instead of accusing you of horrible things, I should have been thanking you." He held out his hand. Deacon hesitated and then he withdrew his hand from Gaby's grasp in order to shake her father's hand. "Gaby tells me that you don't remember much of the accident, but the witness reported that at great risk, you attempted to save my sister."

Deacon visibly swallowed. "I'm sorry for what you've gone through."

"Thank you." Her father's gaze moved to Gaby and then back to Deacon. "As long as you keep my daughter happy, we'll get along just fine."

Gaby glanced around to find that Newton had disappeared. She scanned the crowd for any sign of him. Thankfully she didn't spot him. She hoped he just kept going. The farther away, the better.

When she finally turned back to Deacon, he presented her with a single, perfect red rose. The simple gesture had a profound effect on her heart and love spilled forth.

Gaby lifted up on her tiptoes and looped her arms around his neck. "There's something else I came here to say."

At the same time, they said, "I love you."

As the crowd of onlookers cheered, Gaby leaned into Deacon's embrace. He claimed her lips with a kiss that promised love and happiness.

EPILOGUE

Six months later...

"I NEED TO talk to you." Gabrielle smiled at her new husband in the back of a black limo.

"Really?" The smile he'd been wearing all day slipped from his face. "I wanted to talk to you, too."

"You did?" Gaby sat up straighter. She couldn't imagine what Deacon had on his mind. "Maybe you should go first."

"Wipe that worried look from your beautiful face. Or else I'll have to put up that privacy divider and give you something to smile about." His eyes twinkled with mischief.

She knew exactly what direction her husband's mind had taken and she shook her head as a smile returned to her face. "That will have to wait." When Deacon made a point of pouting, she added, "There's no time. We're almost to the airport."

He nodded in understanding. "As usual, my wife is right."

"Make sure you remember those words the next time we have a disagreement." The lights of the Los Angeles skyline rushed past the window in a blur as their limo headed for LAX. They were hopping a private plane to Fiji. Their honeymoon was going to be a new adventure for the both of them.

"But if we disagree, we get to have make-up sex."

She couldn't help but laugh at her husband's unabashed eagerness. "Do you ever think of anything besides sex?"

"Not when you're around. You've ruined me." He pulled her closer until she was sitting on his lap. Then he closed the divider. "We should probably save Charles from all of this naughty talk. And this way, I can show you what I was thinking about."

He drew her head down to him and claimed her lips with his own. It didn't matter how many times he kissed her, he still made her heart race. His lips moved hungrily over hers, making her insides pool with desire.

She knew where this kiss was headed and it wouldn't leave time for them to talk before the flight. And there were some things they'd put off discussing for too long. It was best to clear the air now before the honeymoon began.

It took every bit of willpower to place her hands on her husband's muscular chest and push back, ending the kiss. "Deacon, wait."

His eyes blinked open and she could read the confusion in his expression. "What's the matter?"

She moved back to the seat beside him. "You're distracting me."

"But in a good way, right?"

"Of course. But we still need to talk."

The color drained from his face. "What's wrong?"

She couldn't help but laugh at the utter look of panic on his face. "Relax. Nothing is wrong."

"You're sure?"

Gaby nodded. "I know we should have talked about this before now, but I was wondering how you felt about children."

"Children?" His gaze narrowed as he eyed her. "I must say I like them. I happened to be one not so long ago."

"Hah! I've seen your six-bay garage with all those sports cars. You're still a kid at heart."

"Busted. But I do make time for business. Speaking of which, remember how I sued *QTR* for that pack of lies they printed about the car accident?"

She nodded. "How's the lawsuit going?"

"It's over. I got the news yesterday, but with the wedding festivities, I didn't want to ruin anything."

Gaby braced herself for bad news. "Did they get it thrown out of court?"

"It never went to court. *QTR*'s board stepped in and between our combined legal teams we hammered out a reasonable deal. The gist of it is they will be revising their editorial guidelines."

Gaby's mouth gaped as she digested the ramifications of the deal. "You mean no more hatchet jobs?"

"Exactly."

"Deacon, that's wonderful." She rewarded him with a kiss, but before it got too heated, she pulled back.

"Why did you stop again? I have a piece of paper that says we must kiss multiple times a day."

She laughed. "I didn't see that on our marriage certificate."

"It's in the fine print."

"Oh. Okay. I'll have to look closer." She smiled. "And did it say anything about how many kids we're supposed to have?"

"No. How many were you thinking?"

"At least one… Since it's already on the way."

For a moment, her husband didn't speak. He didn't move. She wasn't even sure that he was still breathing.

"Deacon, did you hear me?"

"Say it again." His voice lacked emotion and she was beginning to wonder if he was having second thoughts about having children.

"We're having a baby."

"That's what I thought you said." He lifted her back onto his lap. Then he placed his large hand over her abdomen. "You're going to be a mom."

"And you're going to be a dad."

A big smile lit up his eyes. "I love you."

"I love you, too."

She reached out, placing her hand behind her husband's head, and drew him toward her. She claimed his lips with her own. No matter how old she got to be, she would never tire of his kisses. And she planned to grow very old with this wonderful man by her side.

* * * * *

Look out for the next romance story in the
ONCE UPON A FAIRYTALE *duet*

Coming soon!

*And if you enjoyed this story check out these
other great reads from Jennifer Faye*

*SNOWBOUND WITH AN HEIRESS
MARRIED FOR HIS SECRET HEIR
THE MILLIONAIRE'S ROYAL RESCUE
HER FESTIVE BABY BOMBSHELL*

All available now!

Get 2 Free Books,
Plus 2 Free Gifts –
just for trying the *Reader Service!*

READERSERVICE.COM

Manage your account online!

- Review your order history
- Manage your payments
- Update your address

> *We've designed the*
> *Reader Service website*
> *just for you.*

Enjoy all the features!

- Discover new series available to you, and read excerpts from any series.
- Respond to mailings and special monthly offers.
- Browse the Bonus Bucks catalog and online-only exculsives.
- Share your feedback.

Visit us at:
ReaderService.com